The
Secret
General

The Secret General

Stace Woods

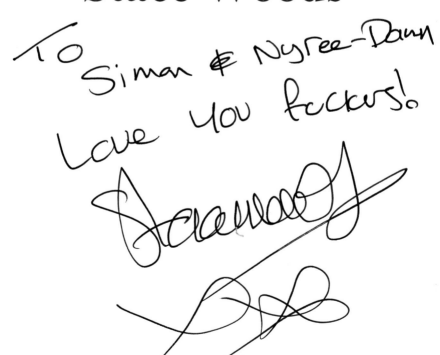

To Simon & Nyree-Dawn
Love you fuckers!

First published in Great Britain in 2021

First edition
Copyright © Stacey McSweeney 2021
The right of Stacey McSweeney, under the
pseudonym Stace Woods, to be identified as the
author of this work has been asserted in
accordance with the Copyright, Designs and
Patents Act 1988.

Set in 13pt Times New Roman

This publication is a work of fiction. All
characters in this novel are fictitious, and any
resemblance to real persons, living or dead, is
purely coincidental.

Dedication

To the amazing people at GG & KC, supporting my kids' education who don't usually get a mention, because they aren't teachers.

Receptionists
Office, admin & finance staff
IT support
Catering staff
Lunchtime supervisors
The cloakroom supervisor
The lollipop lady
Cleaners
Premises staff
TAs
SENCOs
PTAs
MAT
And anyone I may have accidently missed (sorry)

I really appreciate all of your amazing hard work, dedication and commitment.
Thank you.

This book is for you.

"There is no greater agony than bearing an untold story inside you."
- Maya Angelou
I Know Why the Caged Bird Sings

The Secret General

Stace Woods

Prologue

The minibus sped along at forty miles an hour, its stereo blaring. In the back, a group of ten students sang loudly to the song that played on the minibus's CD player. The three teachers in the front, two in the double passenger seat and one in the driver's seat, alternated between laughing and singing along. It had been a good day. They had won the all-girls team netball final, and everyone was in good spirits as the trophy was passed between the singing teenagers.

Marcus Fitzwilliams, or Fitz as he was usually called, loved days like this. As the head of P.E., he often got to see the best and worst in his students. Today, he was seeing them at their very best, and the buzz was incredible. This was why he had become a teacher. He thrived on turning young lives around and helping teenagers reach their full potential. He loved giving them permission to find their strengths and encouraging them to view their weaknesses as a challenge to overcome, rather than something to hold them back.

Not one of these girls could play netball just eighteen months ago. Now they were the district champions. Fitz listened to the excitement in their voices. How proud they all were of each other, was everything to him. As he manoeuvred the minibus through a series of narrow country roads, he smiled broadly to himself. Yes, today was a good day indeed.

The song on the CD player changed, and the students in the back of the minibus began to sing loudly about being champions. Fitz couldn't help but laugh. He felt just as elated as the girls in the back of the bus.

Fitz understood their excitement as he felt it too. He remembered so clearly, the adrenaline, excitement and pride at winning his first district championship when he was at school. His had been for basketball. The fact that he had been so good at basketball hadn't surprised anyone, given his lofty height. What had surprised everyone was when he turned down a basketball career in favour of staying in further education and becoming a P.E. teacher.

He smiled as he thought about that now. He'd never once regretted his choice. He loved giving young people the same encouragement and support he had received as a young man.

"Fitz, you in there?"

"What? Oh, sorry." He had been lost in thought as he drove. His eyes fixed firmly on the road, his thoughts elsewhere entirely.

"I asked if you were still planning to make a pit shop at the upcoming petrol station," Jenny Cribb, one of his fellow P.E. teachers and his girlfriend, asked.

"I'm sorry, babe," he said quietly as he glanced over at her briefly before turning his attention back to the road. "I was miles away. Yes, we'll stop off at the petrol station shortly."

"Where were you?" Jenny asked him. "You were smiling."

"I was thinking back to my first championship win when I was in secondary school."

"Your mum has told me that story so many times," Jenny chuckled.

"Because you've asked her to tell you so many times," Fitz reminded her.

"I know," Jenny mused. "She just beams every time she tells it. She's so proud of you, and I love that story in particular."

"Is it the thought of my big, muscly, black legs in a pair of little shorts?" he asked teasingly.

"Well, I do love those legs," Jenny chuckled.

"Oh god, please make it stop," Clare Knight, the school's netball coach and English teacher, groaned from next to Jenny in the twin front passenger seat. "You two are so sickly; it's repulsive."

"Sorry, Clare," Fitz mumbled, almost shyly. He knew the students in the back wouldn't have heard their conversation over the music, singing, cheers and whoops. He had, however, honestly forgotten that poor Clare was trapped listening to them. His eyes had been focused on the road ahead rather than the front seat, and often, when he spoke to Jenny, it was so easy to forget anyone else was there. They could easily get lost in conversation with each other and block everything else out.

They reached a thirty zone, and Fitz braked gently to slow the minibus down. He travelled for another half a mile, then indicated and pulled into the petrol station on the left-hand side of the road. The three teachers had agreed to stop off at a petrol station to buy drinks and snacks for the students to celebrate their win. It wasn't something that the staff usually did. Still, they were exceptionally proud of their netball team. They felt that they deserved a treat for their fantastic team effort. And for Fitz, it was something his own teachers used to do with his teammates after a big win.

In the back of the minibus, singing, laughing and cheering continued. The trophy did its third round between the girls. It had been repeatedly kissed, hugged and waved in the air and now looked less shiny and a little grubby. As Fitz parked in one of the bays at the petrol station, he called for the girls to all unclip their seatbelts. Everyone unclipped as instructed. Once Fitz got out of the minibus and opened their door, they got out of the van, insisting they take the trophy into the little shop with them, so it couldn't be stolen.

As they all bundled into the shop, the students' singing and cheering continued. The shop was small. Lined with one row of fridges and three rows of shelves. There wasn't room for ten teenagers to be dotted all over it, so Fitz knew it was time to have some order and gather everyone together.

"O.K. ladies, time to settle down," Fitz called over the noise.

The girls immediately quietened down.

"Right," Clare said calmly. "Form an orderly line, ladies. If you stand to the left-hand side of the shop, we won't trample anyone else who comes in."

Without any pushing, shoving, toe stomping or bickering, the group lined up in single file next to the row of fridges and waited patiently for their next set of instructions.

Ten teenage girls in their school sports kits, standing quietly by the fridges, was a sight to behold.

Fitz couldn't help but grin. They were a good bunch, but this was a whole new level of cooperation and engagement. It was amazing what the promise of chocolate could do to a group of teenagers.

"In a moment, I am going to ask each of you to step forward, one at a time," Jenny told the group. "When I do, you will each pick a drink and a sweet or chocolate and a packet of crisps. This is a rare treat for you ladies. You know we don't usually allow you to consume junk food during school hours. Still, you deserve to celebrate your victory today."

The students all politely called out words of thanks to their teachers.

"And remember," Fitz told the squad. "Energy drinks and alcohol are out of bounds. So don't even think about trying to grab a bottle of wine. Especially you two," he added, turning to face Jenny and Clare.

The entire group laughed at Fitz as he mock-scowled at his fellow teachers.

One at a time, the girls picked their snacks, popped them into the baskets Fitz and Jenny were holding and then headed back to the minibus. Clare had already gone back outside, and was waiting for them.

Finally, when everyone else had left the little shop, Fitz turned his attention to Jenny and snaked an arm around her waist. He leant forward slightly and kissed her head.

"Do you have wine at home, or do we need to pick up a bottle?" he asked her.

"Inviting yourself over again, are you?" Jenny teased.

"Well, you're welcome to come back to mine," he shrugged.

"Your school digs?" Jenny asked with a slight chuckle. "No thanks."

"Your place it is then," Fitz said firmly. "Do we need to pick up a bottle or not?"

"I put two in the fridge this morning," Jenny told him. "I was anticipating you breaking the rules and coming over on a school night again."

"I should just move in," Fitz mused. "Then we won't need to keep breaking the 'not on a school night' rule."

"Half of your stuff is already at my flat, and you have a key," Jenny reminded him. "You're right; we should just make it official."

Fitz's heart leapt, and he had to suppress the urge to do a happy dance in the middle of the shop. They'd never really talked about moving in before, and now here they were, talking about it in a petrol station of all places. He pulled Jenny closer and kissed her again.

"Does that mean we are moving in together then?" Jenny asked.

"You bet it does, babe," he said and grinned down at her.

"Good," Jenny said. "Anthony told me he was fed up with you leaving your clutter all over the school."

Fitz knew she was teasing. He prided himself on being very tidy and organised. It wasn't exactly a secret between the school staff that they were together either. However, Anthony Richmond, the headteacher, had never asked Fitz about the possibility of him moving out of his room at the school. They had never talked about Fitz moving in with Jenny. Anthony was too discreet to ask about Fitz's personal life, so Fitz would offer up little bits of information as he and Anthony went for their morning runs. They were as close as brothers, but they still respected each other's right to privacy.

Last to board the minibus were the three teachers. They were met with an eruption of claps, cheers and praise from their students before they set off again.

Fitz's heart swelled with pride and gratitude. These really were remarkable young ladies when they put away their teenage attitudes and let their best selves shine through.

They travelled for about twenty minutes before they were suddenly brought to a halt by a set of temporary traffic lights and a road closure sign. That was odd. There had been no sign of roadworks on the way to the netball match earlier. There hadn't been any signs anywhere on the way back, saying the council had planned to put up a roadblock either.

"Crap," Fitz muttered as he brought the van to a stop and quickly glanced at the directions on the sat-nav to see if it had picked up on the problem and suggested another route. Nothing.

He looked at Jenny and Clare and shrugged.

"Any ideas?" Jenny asked.

"None," Fitz admitted as he looked down and studied the map on the sat nav for a way around the blockade.

Suddenly, the sliding side door on the minibus and the rear doors opened in unison, without warning. Before the three teachers even had the chance to turn around at the sound, screams ricocheted loudly through the bus. The front driver's door and passenger door were pulled open next.

"What the hell?" Fitz yelled as the two women beside him joined the students by letting out their own screams of fear, shock, and panic.

Out of nowhere, the minibus was surrounded by six masked gunmen. They were shouting commands and swearing. The gunmen pulled Fitz and his fellow teachers from the front of the bus. Each teacher was smacked in the back of the legs with a rounders bat, bringing them to their knees. From there, their hands were bound behind their backs, and their mouths were taped shut with silver industrial tape.

One of the gunmen grabbed hold of Fitz's jaw, bent forward and stared right into Fitz's eyes. "Your lot make me sick," he snarled before spitting in Fitz's face. "You shouldn't be allowed out in society. You're fucking filthy, and you make everything around you filthy."

Fitz felt sick. Panic rose inside him almost as quickly as his rage did. Still, he didn't struggle. He didn't react. He didn't dare. He had the lives of the others to think about. He knew if he responded, he could get them all killed. He knew precisely what the gunman was referring to, though.

The gunman didn't like black people.

This wasn't the first time Fitz had been the subject of racist abuse. Over the years, he had been verbally abused by his peers, his students, and even some parents at school. Not at his current school, that was, but at previous schools. There had been many occasions when he had been disrespected as a teacher just because he happened to be black.

One by one, the girls fell silent as they too were bound and gagged in the back of the van. Each teacher was hauled to their feet and slung into the back of the minibus. Their ankles were bound with cable ties and tape.

The girls in the back were crying and struggling, desperate to break free, yet all Fitz could do was watch in horror. He wanted so badly to get them out of this situation, but he knew he would be shot if he even tried to resist. Then there would be no one there with Jenny, Clare and the girls. All he could do was look calm and hope it would help everyone else feel calm.

"Make sure you keep that black scum away from the girls and women," the man who had spat at Fitz called. "We don't want our crop being tainted by him."

Crop?

A nauseating feeling washed over Fitz. This time it had nothing to do with the racist abuse. He'd heard that term used before. It was the way white girls and women were referred to by only one group of men.

S.W.O. Straight Whites Only. A British terrorist organisation, they were determined to overthrow the government. They wanted to rid the U.K. of everyone they considered to be dirty blooded or abominations. They wanted to return women to what they thought to be their rightful place, the kitchen.

Each student and teacher had black hoods placed over their heads. Fitz had to fight the crushing feeling of claustrophobia that he could already feel taking over him. Four of the gunmen climbed into the back of the minibus and closed the doors. The remaining two men quickly threw aside the roadblock they had clearly set up themselves and climbed into the front of the minibus before driving away at speed.

The wording on the side of the minibus read *Surrey Hills All Girls Preparatory School*.

One

Kitty Kline jolted in the driver's seat of her black S.U.V. She shook violently for a few moments. She didn't know what to think or feel. She didn't know how to process what she had just experienced. It shook her at her very core and filled her with dread, panic and crippling fear. Of course, it wasn't the first time she'd had an experience like this, but this one was different. This one had hit her very hard, and this one was a little too close to home. This one was personal. Very personal indeed.

Quickly she scurried out of the vehicle, roughly scooped back her brown curls with her hands and threw up in the road gutter outside her three-bedroom, semi-detached house.

For a brief moment, she just stood there at the kerbside, shaking and unsure what to do. She couldn't catch her breath, and she couldn't focus. Her thoughts and feelings were everywhere as she tried to steady her breathing while what she had just witnessed replayed in her mind's eye.

The warm spring sunshine beamed down on her and bathed her in light. She allowed herself to stand there very briefly and absorb its light, warmth and energy. It washed over her like waves on a beach on a calm sunny day and brought her back into focus.

Within seconds, her training kicked in. She remembered who she was and scrambled to the back of her S.U.V. She pulled open the tailgate and leant into the vehicle's boot compartment. Quickly but carefully, she slid her hand along the bottom of the boot until she found a secret pressure point. This was a fingerprint scanner used to release the boot's false bottom. She put her thumb over the little pad, waited for the beep, pulled the false bottom upwards and locked it locked into place.

Built into the back of her S.U.V. was a remote workstation that she now had full access to. She reached for a sleek black laptop and opened it. Instantly it came out of sleep mode, and she typed the needed password into the prompt box displayed on the screen.

This took her to a second unlock screen. This one requiring her biometric data. She placed her right hand onto a tablet seated next to the laptop and hit the scan option on the computer with her left hand. A red laser light swept across the tablet, scanning her hand before a beep sounded. A green light flashed, and an access granted message appeared on the laptop. Two stages down, two to go.

For the final two stages, she verified her identity with a retina scan and voice authorisation code. Finally, after what seemed like an eternity but was actually less than sixty seconds, she was through to the main home screen on her laptop. She tapped on the icon named "Hub" and, when prompted, typed in her command code. Then as she waited for her video call to connect, she leaned over and reached her tactical vest. The vest was black, Kevlar lined and had holsters for two firearms, four spare clips and two tactical knives for hand to hand combat. She pulled the vest out of its slot in the boot and moved it forward out of the way so she could grab the rest of her uniform. She pulled the three corded crystal pendant necklaces she was wearing off over her head and kicked off her shoes. She grabbed her black cargo trousers and pulled them on, not wasting time by removing the leggings she was wearing first. Then she slipped the rose quartz, amethyst and black obsidian pendants into a small pocket and zipped it closed.

"General Kline." A voice came out of the laptop as the video connected. Thirty-six seconds since she had placed the call. It had felt like an eternity. "We have a situation, Kate," Kitty said as she yanked the trousers over her backside and did them up. She buckled up the belt that she always kept secured in the loops of her waistband to save time, even when she wasn't wearing them. Yanking her light blue floral tunic over her head and revealing the white strappy vest top underneath, she continued, "I had a vision."

"Yes, Ma'am," Kate answered. "Your vitals rocketed. I was analysing the data from the palm scan you just entered, as you called. Your adrenaline is through the roof; do you feel O.K? Any injuries or medical support needed?"

It was an annoying procedure at times, but visions could sometimes be harmful to the psychic witch who received them. The first step after a vision was always to ascertain whether or not they needed medical assistance.

"Fit for duty," Kitty answered, wasting no time by telling Kate that she'd thrown up in the street. She also didn't waste time telling Kate she was still shaking and feeling the pain from being hit in the back of the legs, bound, gagged and dragged thirteen times over. She certainly didn't mention the crippling anxiety that was still causing her to have heart palpitations. She needed to get to Surrey Hills Prep as soon as she could. She needed to check on her own daughters, who were students there.

"Yes, Ma'am," Kate responded. "Your vision Ma'am?"

Kitty pulled on her tight fitted, long-sleeved, black-uniformed t-shirt and socks. At the same time, she recounted the entire vision as quickly as possible. She pulled out her boots and yanked them on hard as she told Kate about Fitz, Jenny, Clare and the ten students who had been taken by S.W.O.

"And you're sure it's Straight Whites Only?" Kate asked.

Kitty nodded. "They were vile to Fitz, the P.E. teacher, because he's black, and they referred to everyone else as their crop. Women and girls who should be home-grown and home kept. They're definitely S.W.O."

"Shit," Kate gasped. "S.W.O. are the most dangerous home-grown terrorists this country has ever faced. If we don't get to them soon, the P.E. teacher will be dead."

"They'll keep him alive for a few hours and have some fun beating the shit out of him," Kitty said. "But we don't have long."

Kitty felt sick. She didn't know Fitz all that well, but she really liked him. He was kind, funny and gentle. She could only imagine what S.W.O. would do to him once they got him to wherever it was they were going. She could still feel the anguish, and dread Fitz had felt when he had realised who he was being abducted by. She could still feel the fear and panic those poor girls were all feeling.

Kitty hated feeling the trauma they were experiencing, and she needed to end it as quickly as she could. She needed to get everyone home safely.

These kids are terrified, Kate," she told her junior as she began to lace and tie the boots. I know some of these girls. I know the teachers. Surrey Hills Prep is my kids' school."

"Oh Shit, Kit, were they on the bus?" Kate asked. Kitty noticed the change in Kate's tone, the abandonment of formality. Their shared friendship coming to the surface.

"No, they don't play netball, thankfully," Kitty assured her. "I had just got in the car to hit the supermarket before the school run, when the vision hit."

Kitty glanced at the laptop screen and saw that Kate was typing furiously. Behind her, she could see two more members of her team on the phone, no doubt alerting the police and MI5, and the final three principal members gearing up to join her in the field.

The warm spring sunshine continued to beam down on her as she laced her boots, surrounding her with a warm glow that was unfitting for the situation she was facing. The situation and her mood were dark and bleak, and the sun's warmth felt like an intruder. Kitty didn't want to be here in glorious sunshine while the hostages were cloaked in darkness in itchy, rancid smelling black hoods.

"Police have been alerted, and armed response units are on the way to the school," Kate confirmed. "We have military and police choppers going up in the air now to scout the location with armed units on their way to the scene. The school has already been notified of a terrorist threat locally and have locked down the building. MI5 is standing by in case we need extra manpower or assistance."

"That's great, thank you. Please make sure Peter Lee is on the scene as soon as possible," Kitty commanded.

"Already alerted and on his way, Ma'am," Kate said.

"Thank you, Major," Kitty said to Kate, and she slammed the laptop closed.

She tied the last bow in her laces and stood once again, grabbing the tactical vest, this time pulling it on. It took her less than a minute to unlock the safe box in the back of her S.U.V., pull out two firearms and click in fully loaded clips into them. She holstered the weapons securely into her vest. She pulled out four spare cartridges fully loaded with bullets, two tactical knives, two pairs of cuffs and two pepper sprays. After that, she pulled out a first aid kit and a handful of medical gloves and finished loading her vest, belt and cargo pockets.

She felt about a stone heavier, but she was geared up and ready to go into the field.

Finally, she grabbed her protective eyewear, snood, helmet and I.D. She secured the false bottom of the boot once again and shut the tailgate before quickly scooping her brown curls in a ponytail. She didn't waste any time undoing the two small plaits and crystals she had tied into her hair that morning that sat on either side of her head, in the middle of all of her thick but tamed curls.

She climbed back into the front of the S.U.V., depositing everything she was not wearing but still needed onto the front passenger seat. She took a mental inventory of all of her equipment and paused briefly to consider anything she may have forgotten. Finally, she was sure she had everything and was ready to go into the field.

She was dreading it. Years of her concealed identity and lifestyle were about to be stripped away once she reached her daughters' school. They had no idea who she really was or what she really did. She had put her twin daughters into that school as it offered accommodation, either full-time or for times of crisis. She loved having her girls around her and so had chosen the emergencies only option. As far as school was concerned, she had a disability that meant she had to stay in hospital from time to time.

The school didn't know that when her girls were required to stay on-site, it was really because she was away on missions. They didn't know that she secretly led a specialist joint MI5-Ministry of Defence taskforce that tracked terrorist threats in the country. They didn't know her witchcraft wasn't just a weird lifestyle choice. They weren't aware she actually had supernatural abilities. She was worried about how they would react when they discovered the truth.

She was worried about how Anthony Richmond would react. She'd been crushing on her kids' headteacher for years. There was obviously no chance of that crush ever developing into anything more. However, she wasn't sure she was ready to tell him she'd been lying to him for years.

Worse, her children were about to discover her deception. Lying to them had been the worst part of her job, but it had been necessary to keep them safe and keep them from worrying about her safety. Now though, their classmates and teachers were in danger, and there was no way she would be able to keep up her lies. She would have to come clean to them too. She just hoped it wouldn't shatter their close bond and that they would be able to forgive her for her deception in time.

She glanced at the clock. 13.46. Shit, six minutes since the vision. There was a time she could have done all of that in three and a half minutes. She cursed herself for not being as fast as she was before her last mission. The stab wound she'd received two months earlier still slowed her down slightly.

It hadn't been a huge mission, but it hadn't gone according to plan, and she had been stabbed in the thigh, the knife nicking her femoral artery. She'd been lucky not to bleed out before help arrived, and although she had recovered well, she was still a little slow on that leg and still struggled to pull it close to her when she pulled on and laced her boots. She still had a slight limp when she ran and occasional pain in her leg, but she was fit for duty and getting stronger every day. She just needed to get her speed back as currently, she wasn't at her best. She was usually O.K with that, but today, it frustrated her and bothered her more than she would like.

There were people that she cared about at risk, and she needed to be better than this if she was going to be able to save them.

She tapped the console near the top of the windscreen with her thumbprint, and a siren started to blare as red and blue lights began to flash. Typically, these lights were discreetly placed within the S.U.V.'s framework so you couldn't see them. Now though, there was no hiding them. Some of her neighbours had already stood there, watching her change clothes in the street. They had frowned and whispered to each other as she loaded weapons about her person. Soon, no one on her road would ever again believe she was just a semi-normal quiet mum.

Two

Kitty had driven these roads many times before. These were her local roads, the ones she took daily to do the school run. Never before had she driven down them at an alarmingly fast speed, though, with lights flashing and sirens blaring. That had always been something she did somewhere else, never in her home town. However, as the details of the vision played over in her mind as she drove, all she could think about was getting to school and making sure her children were safe. She knew they were. She'd already received the call from Kate to confirm that school had been successfully locked down. All students and staff not on the trip were accounted for. In addition to that, local police officers were already on-site and armed response units had started to arrive. The school was safe. Her children were safe. Yet, she knew she wouldn't be able to properly focus on her work until she had seen them for herself.

She needed to hug her daughters and hold them close to her for a moment. Then she would be able to fully focus on her work and bring the hostages home. She had to bring them home. She'd never felt more strongly about rescuing hostages before, and that was something that she was always passionate about. This time though, it was different, more urgent. These hostages were members of her own community. These hostages were people that she knew, and ten of them were children the same age as her own daughters.

The drive to Surrey Hills Prep seemed to take a lifetime, even with it still being an hour before any local schools kicked out, meaning there was less traffic on the road. She was flying over speed humps at fifty miles an hour, and the small amount of traffic on the road was clearing a path for her, allowing her to get through safely at speed. Still, the drive that usually took between ten to fifteen minutes felt like it was taking forever. In truth, though, it had actually only taken three minutes so far to get halfway there. Her personal phone rang, and "Ivy" appeared on the screen of her S.U.V.'s entertainment system. She tapped the answer button.

"Baby, are you O.K.?" Kitty called loudly to her daughter over the blast of the sirens.

"I'm O.K. mum, but school has gone into lockdown. They used the intruder alarm, and we all thought it was just a drill when they put us into lockdown, but there are police here."

She could hear the alarm in her daughter's voice, and she knew she needed to do all she could to reassure her that everything was alright. It wasn't alright at all, but she wanted her daughter to feel calm and safe.

"I know, baby," Kitty told her daughter. "I know all about it, and I promise you are safe. Just hold on, O.K.? I'm going to be there very soon. Then I'll explain everything to you. Is Rosie with you? Is she alright?"

Monday afternoon was music for her twin daughters, and they were in the same music class. They were both learning to play the piano and had been working on a piece they were going to perform together.

"I'm here, Mum," Rosie called. "You're on speaker. We're together in the recording studio."

"Hi baby," Kitty said softly to her daughter. "Are you O.K.?"

"I'm alright, Mum," Rosie answered. "We're just a little confused about what is going on."

"I know you are," Kitty told her daughter. "As soon as I have seen Mr Richmond, I am going to explain everything to you, and it'll all make sense. For now, though, just know that you are safe."

"There's no way they are going to let you in if you come, Mum. The police will never let you through the door," Ivy called.

"It's O.K.," Kitty assured her daughters. "I can't explain it right now, but I can assure you that I will be allowed in."

Kitty slowed, indicated, checked her mirrors and turned left at a corner. She rechecked her surroundings, saw it was safe and sped up once more. She was getting close now. She wouldn't be able to see her children instantly, but she knew she would feel that much better just being in the same building as them.

She briefly glanced up at the sky. It was a beautiful shade of blue with just a few fluffy clouds dotted around. When her daughters were little, they used to think clouds like this were magic sheep flying in the sky. She chuckled softly to herself. Her S.U.V.'s sirens were still blaring from the outside. She had her windows closed to drown out enough of the noise that she could still hear her daughters, so long as she had the volume on the S.U.V.s entertainment system cranked right up.

She slowed, indicated, checked her mirrors again and turned another corner. She kept her eyes firmly on the road ahead as other vehicles moved out of her way and allowed her to pass them quickly. She was just two minutes away from her daughters now and a knot formed in her belly. She hadn't felt anxiety like this in years, and now it was threatening to consume her.

"Mum," Rosie interrupted Kitty's thoughts "Are you driving? Why are there such loud sirens? Are you here already? And how did you even find about this before we called? We only went into lockdown less than ten minutes ago."

"Girls, I am going to be in the building within the next few minutes. I really must see the head, and then I'll explain everything to you, I promise. It'll all make sense soon."

"They won't let you in, Mum," her twin daughters said in unison.

Kitty was never sure if it was a twin thing or a teen thing when they did that these days, but it made her smile.

"Girls, there are things about me that you don't know," Kitty told her twins. "You're about to find out everything, though. When you do, just remember that I am still your mother, I love you, and I never wanted for you to find out this way."

"Mum, are you in trouble?" Rosie asked. "You're worrying us."

"Not in the least," Kitty reassured her girls.

"Mum," Ivy said, in her 'I'm not convinced' tone.

"Girls, I promise you. I'm in no trouble. Please just trust me. I'll explain everything. Soon it will all make sense."

"You're scaring us," Ivy said.

"We're freaking out, Mum," Rosie admitted."

"It's O.K., girls," Kitty reassured her daughters. "I promise you're safe, and I promise everything is going to make so much sense soon. Your mum is a bad arse. I need to ring off now, though. Just sit tight and wait for me. I promise I'll be with you as soon as I can. I love you."

"Love you too, Mum," the girls said together. "See you soon."

Kitty clicked the hang-up button as she slowed right down. She was approaching the school and needed to pull up at the front gates and show her I.D. There was no longer any avoiding it. She would have to tell her daughters the truth about who she really was and what she really did. Very soon, they were going to know the truth. How would they react? Would they be angry? Would the truth damage their relationship? Would they ever forgive her for all the years of lying and deception?

As she reached the turning for the gate, she turned off the siren but left her lights flashing. An armed police officer approached her as she pulled up at the gate. She unwound her window and held out her I.D. to the officer.

"General Kline," she told him. "I'm running this operation."

"General?" He asked sceptically.

"Yes, Constable," She confirmed. "General."

"Forgive me, General, but you seem a little young for the rank," The officer responded. "Given the nature of the incident, I'm going to have to verify your identity."

"Thank you, Officer," she said politely. "Is the Chief Superintendent here yet? Radio him and tell him I'm here, would you? We've worked together before; he'll vouch for me."

"Yes, Ma'am," The officer said, and he got onto his radio, still clutching Kitty's I.D.

Usually, Kitty wouldn't mind being held under suspicion. She usually welcomed it, in fact. She appreciated officers who questioned her and were cautious about a thirty-seven-year-old woman claiming to hold the rank of General. If her division wasn't so specialist and her abilities so rare, she would never have made it to General at this stage in her career. Today though, she just wanted to yell, "Get the fuck out of my way," so she could get to her kids.

Of course, she didn't do that. She sat patiently and waited for the P.C. to finish on his radio. Once he did, he apologised and handed back Kitty's I.D. and let her through. As she pulled up outside the building, Chief Superintendent Peter Lee was at the door waiting for her. She turned off the engine, stepped out of the S.U.V., closed the door and pocketed her keys.

"Kitty," Peter said warmly as she got out of her S.U.V. "You alright?"

"I'm alright, thanks, Sir, you?" She responded with a smile.

"Don't start that bullshit," Peter told her firmly but still smiling. "We both know the Army is well in my past, and you didn't call me Sir when we were digging into our Sunday lunch yesterday.

"Fair enough," She said, grinning.

There was something about being around Peter that helped her to relax a little. He'd been her commanding officer when she'd been in the Army. We was like a big brother to her. He'd been a constant presence in her life after she'd left the Army to raise her family, particularly after her husband Jack had died.

He was over six feet, athletic and still had a cropped military haircut, even in his late forties. These days his blonde hair was speckled with grey. His wife said it made him look like he was maturing like a fine wine, so he had embraced the grey, and Kitty loved him for it. She was glad he had lived to an age where grey was even a thing. Not everyone they had served with had been that lucky, her own husband included.

"So, what's the plan?" Peter asked as they turned and began to walk up the stone steps that led to the school's entrance.

"For now," she answered. "The plan is to see the headteacher and see my girls. I have a lot of explaining to do while I wait for my team to chopper in."

"What can I do?" Peter asked, patting her back gently as they walked.

"As desperately as I want to see my daughters, I need to see the headteacher first," she admitted. "Do you think you could please arrange for the girls to have a secure escort to a quiet place for me to talk to them?"

"I'll fetch them for you myself," he assured her. "It'll give me a chance to say hi to the terrible two. No one is in the office next to the head's if you want to use it. I'll take the girls to wait for you in there. I have already asked the head to wait in his office for the operations commander to meet with him privately."

"Thank you," Kitty said as they made their way into the school building. "I'll join you and the girls in there just as soon as I can. I'm dreading having to come clean."

"They'll be alright," Peter told her. "They take after you and Jack. They'll accept it as it is and move on."

"I hope you're right," Kitty said, trying to smile but unsure of how convincing she was.

Kitty stopped just inside the doors and looked around. The walls were all adorned with solid oak panelling and framed photos, and the floors were carpeted in light grey. The building was over one hundred and fifty years old, and she had been visiting it frequently for seven years. Today though, it all felt brand new. She was seeing it differently, experiencing it from a tactical point of view, taking in every detail as if she were seeing it all for the first time.

The reception, admin and office support staff were waiting in a small office next to the main reception area to the left of them. When Kitty walked into the room freely, they all turned and stared at her. It was time to face the first hurdle. A sea of angry faces looked at her. She stood there for a moment, her shoulders back and her chin up, taking in their pissed-off expressions.

"Miss Kline," the office manager said. "You really shouldn't be here."

Kitty could hear the hostility in the woman's voice. She'd never much liked Kitty and had always looked down her nose at her. It amused Kitty that this woman was so judgemental when she didn't know the first thing about who Kitty was.

"What the hell?" the receptionist gasped, noticing the holstered guns Kitty was wearing. "Have you really come onto school premises wearing guns? What is wrong with you?"

Kitty stared at her. This woman was usually really agreeable and friendly. She'd never heard her even sound remotely annoyed before now. Peter appeared and side-stepped around Kitty. She looked at him and smirked slightly. She ignored the tutting sounds coming from the ladies standing opposite her.

"I trust you all know General Kline," he said by way of an ice breaker.

"Gen-General?" The office manager stammered. "Bu-but…"

"General Kline's true identity has been a closely guarded secret for a long time," he interrupted before adding, "As a matter of national security." Everyone in the room just stood there in shocked silence, a few nodding their heads slightly.

"And that's how it needs to remain," Kitty said firmly. "This is a major operation, and I must ask all of you to refrain from discussing this with anyone. A team of police officers will take command of your phones and answer all calls for the foreseeable future. I need you to all wait here and talk to no one other than those present in this room at this time."

More nodding and a few words of agreement were mumbled from the ladies standing in the office, but Kitty could see their eyes burning into her. They did not look happy.

"My team will be here shortly," Kitty continued. "When they arrive, they are going to need the meeting room to set up a command centre. Once that is done, we will brief all of the staff and explain the situation. For now, though, I need to see Anthony and go through everything with him first."

With that, Kitty turned on her heel and walked out of the small office, still amused by the frosty reception she had received. She made her way down the corridor toward Anthony Richmond's office. The panelled walls were adorned with large, framed photos of students and teachers involved in various educational and extra-curricular activities. Kitty tried to focus on each image as she passed it. She was desperate to focus on anything other than the conversation she was just about to have with her kids' headteacher. She'd never really paid much attention to the photos before. Still, today she walked slowly and deliberately, taking in as much detail as possible. She didn't want to think about the conversation she was about to have. Not only was Anthony about to learn the truth about her identity, but she was also about to tell him that thirteen of his people had been taken hostage. Worse, she couldn't tell him why. She had no answers to give him about any of it at this stage. She didn't know where they were or why they had been taken. At this stage, all she knew was what she had experienced in her vision.

All too soon, she was standing outside his door.
She was about to turn his world upside-down, and
the dynamic of their relationship was about to be
forever changed. She flashed her I.D. to the
police officer standing outside the office and
knocked on the door.
She paused to take a few steadying breaths and
tried to steady her nerves.
"This is ridiculous," she scorned herself quietly.
She'd been involved in dangerous conflicts all
over the world. She'd even served on the front
lines in Afghanistan and Iraq. Why the hell was
she so anxious about one conversation with one
ordinary man?
"Come in," She heard a familiar voice say.
Kitty took one more breath and opened the door.

Three

Kitty walked into the room and looked at Anthony Richmond, the head teacher of Surrey Hills Prep. As she stared at him, an all too familiar feeling of butterflies bursting into life formed in the pit of her tummy. He really was incredibly handsome. He was six feet four inches, had a well-muscled physique that his black suit couldn't hide and thick black, wavy hair that she always wanted to run her hands through. His silver-grey eyes always seemed to sparkle with mischief, despite his professional manner. This man was her weakness. Being in his office made it worse as the sweet smell of his aftershave lingered in the room and tickled her senses. He was seriously sexy, and she found it hard to concentrate just being in the same room as him. His head was down, and he was shuffling through some papers on his oversized mahogany desk. Kitty shut the door behind her and cleared her throat loudly. It was time to face the music. Anthony looked up, surprise evident on his face. "Kitty," he said, a hint of annoyance in his usually cheerful tone. "I'm sorry, but you really shouldn't be here right now. It's highly inappropriate."

"Actually," she corrected him. "Here is exactly where I need to be. Right now, I need to be right here with you in this room."

She liked it even less than he did, but he needed to know what had happened to his people. He needed to know that she would be the one leading the team that was going to try to rescue them.

"I'm sorry, Kitty," he said, sounding more displeased than sorry, "I'm waiting for-"

"Me," she finished. "You're waiting for me." She crossed the room and stood in front of his desk. *That's it, Kitty*, she thought. *Nice and confident. You are in command here. You are in control. Make him pay attention.*

Now though, Anthony looked angry. She hadn't even told him anything yet, and he was already pissed off. Not a good start.

He stood. "Are you shitting me right now?" he demanded hotly.

Kitty blinked in amazement. In seven years, she had never heard her kids' headteacher mutter anything close to a curse word. She was stunned. "Excuse me?" She asked. She was genuinely confused as to why he was already so angry with her.

"We're in the middle of a police enforced lockdown, and you're in here flirting with me? How the hell did you even get in here?"

Before she had the opportunity to answer him, he had crossed the room and had his hand firmly but not painfully gripped around her elbow.

"Flirting," she hissed. "You think I'm here to flirt?"

Anthony didn't respond. Instead, he marched her across the room and opened the door. He led her into the corridor where the police officer she had seen on her way in was still keeping watch.

"Please remove Miss Kline from the premises," Anthony said impatiently as he released his grip on her elbow. "She's welcome to come back and talk when the situation is more under control, but we have policies in place and parents are not allowed in the building during lockdown procedures."

The officer turned to Kitty.

"Is everything alright, General? Can I assist you?"

"No, that's O.K., thank you, Officer," Kitty said. "Everything is absolutely fine. There just seems to be some miscommunication between myself and Mr Richmond."

"I see, General," the officer said.

"Also," she said sarcastically. "Mr Richmond seems to have overlooked the fact that I came to school today packing heat. You'd have thought he might have noticed that by now."

Anthony looked from the officer to Kitty to the body armour and guns she was carrying. He stared at her, the disbelief evident on his face.

"What the hell is going on?" he demanded hotly.

"I will explain everything," she said more softly.
"If we can just return to your office. And quickly
please, my team has a major terrorist incident to
deal with and, I need to explain everything to you
as quickly as I can."

"Your team?" he asked, still obviously confused.
"General? What?"

"Your office," she said more firmly this time.
Anthony shared at the guns she was wearing one
more time before he turned and headed back into
his office. Kitty followed and once again closed
the door.

"General?" he asked, turning to look at her.

"General," she repeated, taking out her I.D. and
handing it to him.

He studied it carefully before staring at Kitty and
then back at her I.D card.

"But you don't work," he said. You're too sick.
The local authority funds your kids' placements
here because of your bad health, and a school that
offers emergency board is the only way to keep
the girls out of foster care every time you have to
be admitted to the hospital. How can you possibly
have a M.O.D identity card that says you are a
General?"

Oh boy, he was not handling this very well at all,
and she hadn't even told him about the hostage
situation yet.

"Actually," she said, moving around him to take an uninvited seat at the round table positioned at the top end of his office," The Crown Purse funds the girls' placements here. I work for Her Majesty as part of a joint sub-division of MI5 and the M.O.D."

She waved her hand toward one of the brown leather tub chairs positioned around the table as if she was inviting him to sit down in his own office. In any other situation, she might have found that rather funny. There was nothing funny about what was happening now, though.

"But your long stints in hospital," he said.

"Undercover assignments," she shrugged.

"We brought the girls to visit you in the hospital twice when you needed surgery."

"I got shot," she said simply. "And then knifed."

"But…"

She cut him off with a dismissive wave of her hand.

"Anthony, we don't have time for this," she said impatiently. "There are lives at stake. My command team will be here anytime, and we have a major incident to discuss.

"What incident?" Anthony asked. He finally took a seat at the table and leant back in his chair.

"There is no way for me to sugar-coat this, Anthony," Kitty warned. "But I have some bad news to share with you."

"Just spit it out, Kitty," Anthony demanded.

Clearly, he was in no mood to entertain good manners or practice patience today. She wasted no further time and came right out and said what needed to be said. She felt sick before the words even left her mouth but now was finally the time to be honest.

"At approximate thirteen-forty hours, the minibus carrying your students and staff back from their netball tournament was intercepted by six armed terrorists. Everyone on board was taken hostage at gunpoint."

"Is this some kind of sick joke?" Anthony roared, pushing his chair away from the table and getting back on his feet. "What the hell is wrong with you, Kitty? Why would you come in here and say something like that?"

Kitty followed suit and stood up. She placed the palms of her hands on the mahogany table, her short manicured nails on display.

"Anthony look at me," she instructed, keeping her voice low and her tone calm. "Look at my face. Do I look like I'm lying to you?"

"You've been lying to me for years Kitty," Anthony shot. "How can you expect me to believe anything you say when you are clearly a professional liar."

"Anthony," she said again. She kept the same tone in her voice but spoke a little louder this time. She needed to defuse this situation quickly. She needed Anthony to calm down and get on board.

He was a good, kind-hearted man. He was always in control of himself, and he was always respectful. She understood this new side of him completely, but she needed calm and collected Anthony back in the room.

"What happened to them?" he asked finally, rubbing his temples.

"They were taken by the terrorist organisation Straight White Only."

Anthony sank back in his chair. Kitty also sat back down and leant back in the chair, clasping her hands in her lap.

"Fitz," he whispered.

Kitty nodded.

Neither of them needed to say anything more than that. Fitz was a black man who had been taken hostage by white supremacists. He was in grave danger.

"How do you know all of this?" he asked warily.

"That I can't answer," she said cautiously. "There are still parts of my identity that I must protect."

"I have thirteen missing people, General, including ten kids, and you are worried about your identity." He was so angry, he was almost shouting at her.

"You need to understand something, Anthony," she said hotly, rising to her feet once more. She noticed his eyes were once again drawn to the guns she was wearing. She was feeling too hot-headed and impatient to care that he looked so distressed.

"My job doesn't fall down to this one fucking awful incident," she snapped. "My role means protecting Queen and country. There will always be incidents like this. They are awful and scary, and I am sorry this has happened to you, but I cannot give you any more information at this point. I risk my life and my children growing up without a mother to do my job. The more people here know all of the details, the more this school and my children are in danger."

Anthony leant back in the leather upholstered chair and nodded.

"I'm sorry," he said after a few moments. "I understand."

He beckoned toward the chair, and she sat again.

"You have no idea how much I wish I could tell you everything," she whispered, leaning across the table and taking his hand in hers. "But I won't make you, my kids or this school a target by people knowing too much. As it is, every adult here will have to sign documents that will hold them legally bound to The Official Secrets Act. It's also important that no students other than my own daughters see me like this."

She waved a hand in front of herself, highlighting the uniform and the guns.

"Do they know?" Anthony asked. "Do the girls know who you really are?"

Kitty cast her eyes downward and stared at the table. "They have no idea, and in a few minutes, I have to go and tell them the truth. That their mother works for a secret government organisation that catches terrorists."

"Tell me what I can do," Anthony said softly as he squeezed her hand gently before releasing it and standing once again.

"I need the full records of the students and teachers on that minibus. I'll also need your personal observations about Fitz, Clare and Jenny, especially Fitz."

He nodded. "Of course," he said. "What else?"

"I need to know how many students are due to leave the property today and how many are boarding. I need to know exactly what's been said to any parents who have phoned about this lockdown situation. I will be arranging military protection for all students who remain on-site. My team will be writing a press statement that you will have to share. I will also need to you allow us to retain control of the school's phone lines as the terrorists may call here with demands. Staff are still welcome to use the phones for internal calls only."

Anthony sighed sadly. "You can have anything you need, General. I'll do anything to get my people back here safe and well."

"Good," she said. "And one more thing, I need to you just call me Kitty. I may be leading this operation, but I need us to have the same dynamic we've always had for this to work. It's important that if any students see me here, they see me just as another parent."

Anthony nodded again, and Kitty nodded back, mirroring his actions.

"I agree," he said firmly. "But you might want to lose the guns."

After Kitty had left his office, Anthony began to pace the room. He felt like a complete jerk. He'd just yelled at a parent, sworn at them and generally been out of control. This wasn't how he usually behaved, and he hadn't made a very good impression.

He realised he needed a few moments to calm himself, gather his thoughts and get back into headteacher mode before facing anyone else. Otherwise, he was likely to continue to be an arse to everyone around him, and that wasn't how he operated. It certainly wasn't how he operated around Kitty.

She'd played a clever little game for seven years, leading him to believe that she had some serious undisclosed medical condition. All the time, though she'd actually been a government agent. He was angry, but that anger would have to be pushed aside if he was going to let her do her job and bring his staff and students back alive. He knew that. Yet, he also knew she had purposefully deceived him, and he had fallen for it. What an idiot.

Still, despite his better judgement, he liked Kitty. He still liked her far more than was appropriate. Being angry at her hurt him, but it was better to be pissed off than be distracted by the lustful feelings he'd had for her for the past seven years. Right now, he needed to bury those feelings as far down as he could, and he wasn't sure he would be able to do that if he didn't let himself be angry at her. How could he be pissed, though, without his foul mood following him like a dark cloud, rubbing off on those around him?

He felt conflicted and angry with himself. He knew he shouldn't let Kitty get under his skin like that. He knew he should be able to be professional and block off his feelings for her. However, he also knew when she stood there, in all of her tactical gear, he found her undeniably sexy. Sexier than he had ever found her before, and he hadn't thought that was possible.

The phone on his desk began to ring. He could tell by the ringing sound that it was an internal call, and he crossed the room and stood behind his desk before picking up the receiver.

"Anthony here," he said as he answered the phone, trying to sound cheerier than he felt.

"I just wanted to give you a heads up that Kitty's task force have arrived and are beginning to set up in the meeting room. I still have no idea what is happening or if they are welcome guests, so I wanted to check you are O.K. with us offering them refreshments."

"Thanks, Libby," Anthony responded. "They are most welcome and most needed at this time, so please do offer them some refreshments and any support and cooperation they need. I'll head out in just a moment."

"I understand," Libby said." I'll make sure everyone here knows to give the task force anything they need."

"Great," Anthony said. "I'll see you in a couple of minutes."

Anthony replaced the receiver and sat down. He pulled out a new notebook from his desk drawer and quickly jotted down the list of things Kitty had asked for. He usually loved starting a new notebook. It helped him to feel organised and gave him a small dopamine rush. Not this time, though. This time it served to remind him that lives were at stake.

After everything was over, he would give the notebook to Kitty and allow her to do what she wanted with it. For now, though, he needed to make sure he was staying on top of things. On the second page, he made a list of things that he needed to do that Kitty had asked for. On the next, he listed everything else that would need to be done to maintain the effective operation of the school. He jotted thoughts such as asking extra staff to stay at school and asking the catering team to provide evening meals and snacks for Kitty's task force and the police officers on-site. And, of course, he needed to make contact with the families of the hostages. He would invite them into school. They would need refreshments, meals and staff support too.

He stood with his notebook and pen in hand, walked around his desk and left the room, switching the lights off on his way out. It was time to work with Kitty's team and make the phone calls he was dreading.

Four

There was only one conversation Kitty was dreading more than the conversation with Anthony and that as the conversation with her daughters. All in all, Anthony was quite reasonable and accepting of her years of deception. Yes, he had been shocked and worked up and understandably upset when he learnt of his missing staff and students, but all in all, he had been quite reasonable. O.K, he'd been furious, but it really could have been worse. Now Kitty was sure worse about to come.

Once again, she was standing outside an office door, trying to get the nerve to go in. She could hear chatter coming from the room inside. Peter was laughing, and so were the twins. They were happy and upbeat, and any hint of fear that had been evident earlier had vanished from their voices. Rosie and Ivy had always been close to Peter. He was right by her side when the twins were delivered by elective caesarean section, and he'd been a constant presence in their lives ever since.

As Kitty stood outside the office, she turned to look back at Anthony's office. She could still smell his aftershave, teasing her. It wasn't an overpowering smell, and she was sure the corridor didn't usually smell of it. It probably wasn't even lingering in the air or on her at all. Yet she could remember exactly how it smelt, and the scent was as fresh to her now as it had been when she'd been sitting in his office moments earlier.

She'd never seen him visibly upset before, and it had hurt her to know that she had inflicted so much pain on him. Not directly, she knew. It wasn't her fault that his people had been taken hostage, but it was she who had delivered the shocking and distressing news. It was she who had spent seven years lying to him. It was she who had broken the news that Fitz was now in the hands of white supremacists. Yes, Kitty had inflicted much pain on him just now, and now she was about to inflict the same pain on her own children.

Kitty took hold of the brass door handle of the office her daughters were in with Peter and went inside.

"Mum," the girls gasped in unison.

"What are you wearing?" Ivy asked.

"Crap, Mum," Rosie added. "They're guns!"

Her girls shocked expressions amused Kitty. It had been a long time since she'd been able to surprise her kids.

"Thanks," she chuckled. "I'd never have noticed that all by myself."

Kitty put her arms out, and her girls rushed into them.

"Do not touch the weapons," She ordered as her girls hugged her fiercely.

God, it felt so good to have her daughters in her arms and see for herself that they were safe and well. Of course, she had known they were safe, but she had still needed to see them to really feel it. It was one of those things that she knew all the school mums would be feeling that afternoon. All of them, aside from the mums whose children she needed to find and bring home. She couldn't imagine what they would be feeling. She hugged her daughters tighter still, desperately thankful that they had never expressed an interest in netball. Desperately grateful that they were safe at school and not two of the ten kids who were now missing.

She felt their warmth against her, inhaled the sweet apple smell of their shampoo and closed her eyes. She had her daughters in her arms. They were safe, and she was blessed.

"What's going on, Mum?" Rosie asked as both girls pulled back and looked up at their mother.

"I'm going to explain everything," Kitty assured her two daughters.

She looked at her girls. At five foot ten inches, Kitty was still six inches taller than the twins. Today though, they felt even smaller than that. They felt like little girls, and she wanted desperately to protect them. She remembered how they had looked as toddlers with cute little blonde pigtails and matching dresses. Now they had thick manes of silky blonde hair cascading down their backs and matching green and red tartan school skirts. They weren't babies anymore, and she knew she couldn't protect them from the truth any longer. It was time to tell them everything.

"I'll step outside and leave you ladies to it," Peter said, stepping away.

"Thanks, Peter," Kitty said.

"Hey, look at that," He beamed. "You can do it."

"Thank you, Sir," Kitty corrected sarcastically. He rolled his eyes.

"Are you sure our mum isn't in trouble, Uncle Pete?" Ivy suddenly implored Peter.

"I Promise," Peter said. "Your mum is going to tell you everything. Just remember, whatever she tells you, your mum is a hero."

Ivy nodded and smiled, looking reassured, and Peter left the room.

"Sit down, girls," Kitty said as she walked over to the heavy oak desk and sat down behind it in the teacher's chair. She motioned for the girls to sit in the other two chairs where students or parents usually sat. Ivy and Rosie sat, and once again, Kitty pulled out her I.D. She set it down on the desk between her daughters, and they leant forward and looked at it together.

Well, she had made a start. There was no going back now. The truth was beginning to come out. Her daughters were studying her I.D with confused expressions, but at least they didn't look angry.

"General?" They asked together.

"As in the Army?" Rosie asked.

"I thought you left the Army before you were pregnant with us," Ivy said.

"I did," Kitty confirmed. "I'm not exactly Army anymore. I work for another organisation that works with the Army."

"Is this why you have to keep going away, and we have to stay here sometimes?" Ivy asked.

"Yes," Kitty confessed. "It Is."

"What exactly is it you do, Mum?" Rosie asked.

"I lead a specialist counter-terrorism task force," Kitty said honestly. She left out the part about her supernatural powers and working with witches. There was only so much she had time to tell the girls right now. She would tell them the truth about the rest when all of this was over.

"And Uncle Pete," Ivy began. "He said you're a hero."

"I wouldn't call myself a hero," Kitty said.

"But you've saved lives." Rosie pressed.

"Yes," Kitty said.

"Lots of lives?" Ivy asked.

"Yes," Kitty said simply. She didn't want to overdramatise her role. She worked with many amazing people who had saved lots of lives. It wasn't just her.

"Then you're a hero," both girls said.

"Why didn't you tell us?" Ivy asked.

"Because you knowing puts you in danger," Kitty told her daughters honestly.

"So we're in danger now?" Ivy asked.

"I really hope not, but there is a chance that everyone here is in danger right now," Kitty said honestly. "We think bad people have targeted this school because of the wealth and importance of some of the families here. They think it'll make it more likely for them to have their demands met."

"Not us then," Said Ivy.

"Yes, you," Kitty corrected. "You didn't know it, but my job is very important. If anyone was to find out that you are the daughters of the General of a counter-terrorism task force, you could become targets."

"Wow." Once again, Kitty's daughters' were speaking in tandem.

"That's scary, Mum," Ivy said.

"But you have the coolest job," Rosie added, and Ivy nodded in agreement.

Kitty looked at them and smiled proudly. She was so amazed by her daughters. They could have ranted and raved at their mother. They could have yelled and made accusations. But they didn't. They just sat there, calmly asking questions. Intelligent questions. Seeking the facts and telling her that she was a hero. They were her heroes. Her two precious girls weren't angry, just curious and supportive. They were so much like Jack, and she loved them all the more for it.

"What happened, today Mum?" Ivy asked. "Why are we in lockdown, and why are you dressed like Lara Croft?"

Kitty chuckled softly. It had been her turn to pick the family movie on Saturday night, and she had decided to introduce her kids to Tomb Raider. Finally, she sighed and answered.

"Three teachers and ten students were abducted by terrorists a little while ago." Kitty said, deciding honesty was the best policy.

"Who?" Ivy asked.

"Do you know why?" Rosie added.

"Honestly, I'm not completely sure why yet," Kitty admitted. "I have a couple of theories, but I can't share them right now. As for who, it's the year eight netball team, Miss Cribb, Miss Knight and Mr Fitzwilliams."

"Oh my god," the girls gasped together.

"Those are our friends Mum," Rosie said.

"And our teachers," Ivy chimed in.

"I know, darlings," Kitty sighed. "I'm so sorry."

Kitty decided no further details or specifics would help her girls to process what was going on. She didn't want her kids to know what extra danger their P.E teacher was facing simply for being a black man. Therefore, she had purposely chosen to omit the part about the terrorists being S.W.O.

Fitz was a gentle giant, and all of the kids at school loved him. It wouldn't benefit her children to know he was probably being beaten to a pulp at that very moment.

"Are they going to be alight, Mum?" Rosie asked.

"Are you going to save them?" Ivy added.

Kitty looked at her daughters sat at the other side of the desk, and her heart broke. Tears streamed down their cheeks, and they were trembling. Her daughters were frightened, but soon the whole school would know what was happening, and she wanted them to hear about it from her and not a classmate.

"I'm going to do my very best, girls, I promise," she assured her daughters. "I'm so sorry this has happened, and I am so sorry that I can't sit with you and support you while all of this is going on. I have to coordinate the search and rescue of your friends and teachers. My team should be here now, and I have to work with them to get everyone home safely. If you need anything, though, you can just text me, and I'll get back to you as soon as I can."

"We understand, Mum," Ivy said. "We know you have to go to work now and find our friends."

"I do," Kitty said. "But know that I love you, and I am thinking of you."

"Your job," Rosie said suddenly. "Does it have something to do with you being a witch?"

"Yes," Kitty said. "But let's just keep that between ourselves for now. Not many people know that, and I will explain it all to you properly when this is all over."

Her kids knew that she was a witch, did spell work, and worked with nature and energy of the moon. They didn't realise that supernatural powers existed, though. They didn't know she could control the elements or that Kate from her team could blow things up with her mind.

"Not many people know much about your real job at all, do they?" Ivy asked.

"No, they don't, Kitty said."

"But Uncle Pete does?" Rosie asked.

"Uncle Pete does," Kitty confirmed. "He is always close by when I am working away, keeping an eye on you."

As if by magic, the door knocked, and Peter walked into the office. Kitty was sure he had a sixth sense and knew when she was talking about him. It wasn't the first time he'd appeared, just as she'd mentioned his name.

"Sorry to bother you, Kitty, but your team has arrived," he said.

Kitty nodded. "I'm sorry, girls, but I really need to get to work now."

"You're going to find our friends aren't you, Mum? Ivy asked.

"And our teachers," Rosie added.

"I promise you both," Kitty said. "I am going to try my very hardest to find them and bring them home safely."

"We know you will, Mum," Ivy said. "You never let us down."

"Well then," Kitty said, rising to her feet. "I had better not start letting you down now."

It was true that she always tried hard not to let the twins down. There had been occasions when she hadn't been able to attend events with them or had to cancel plans at the last minute because of assignments. Still, her girls had never viewed that as being let down. They were always too excited about spending time with Uncle Pete and Aunt Sarah, which usually involved ice cream, ice staking and pizza.

Kitty didn't want to have to pull herself away from her daughters, but she knew she would have to so she could get cracking on finding the S.W.O terrorists and their hostages. She was just still amazed that they hadn't been upset by her years of lying and secret-keeping. Instead, they just understood and wanted to support her.

At last, she got to her feet, walked back around the desk and stood in front of her girls. They stood, and she hugged them once more and left the room.

"Our Mum's a hero," Rosie told Peter as he walked around the desk to occupy the seat Kitty had just vacated.

"I know she is girls," he said. "I know."

Five

It had been over an hour since Kitty's vision. She had learnt over the years the different sensations different visions left her with. Past, present and future visions all felt different as she received them. She knew the vision of her daughters' classmates being abducted happened at the exact moment she saw it.

She still had the residual pain in her legs, knots in her stomach and could feel the fear the hostages had felt ricocheting through her. She could still smell the dirty black hoods placed over the victims' heads, could still feel the panic at not being able to breathe properly, and the terrifying feeling of claustrophobia from being bound, gagged and hooded. She found that she kept rubbing her wrists from the pain of the cable ties that the hostages had been bound with.

To make it worse, she could still see the look of anguish on Anthony's face as she had told him what had happened. She cared about him deeply, too deeply, if she was honest with herself and couldn't stand the thought that she had hurt him.

It wasn't her fault, and she knew that, but still, she had caused him pain. In her mind, being the weird school mum with a big crush on the headteacher was terrible enough. Now her personal and professional lives were colliding in a big way, and honestly, she wasn't sure how to cope with that.

This wasn't the first time her psychic abilities and her personal life had collided so dramatically. Kitty had told her parents about her visions and the accompanying physical ailments that came with them as a child. Of course, they hadn't believed her, and after telling them several times throughout her childhood and each time them looking at her as if she was crazy, she stopped telling them. That was, of course, until Uncle Tim.

Tim had been Kitty's mother's brother. She had been sixteen and had been helping her mother in the kitchen when the vision came. She had screamed and dropped the salad bowl she was holding, sending it smashing across the kitchen floor. There was blood. God, there was so much blood. Not hers, of course, but in her mind's eye, she could see the blood seeping out of Uncle Tim's broken body.

She could smell it. She could taste it as it tricked out of his mouth. That unmistakable iron-rich, metallic taste of blood had made her gag.

She'd crouched on the floor, surrounded by the shattered glass, screaming and rocking. Her mother, who was thankfully wearing shoes, clambered over the broken glass, pulled Kitty up to her feet, and held her in her arms.

"He's gone," Kitty cried. "Uncle Tim's gone."

"Not this again, Kitty," her mother sighed. "How many more times are we going to do this?"

"Listen to me, Mum," Kitty had screamed. "Uncle Tim is dead."

"STOP IT!" Her mother had yelled. "STOP IT RIGHT NOW!"

Kitty had shoved her mother out of the way and ran to the phone. She picked up the receiver and dialled Uncle Tim's number. It rang and rang with no answer.

Kitty looked at her mother.

"We have to go now, Mum," Kitty pleaded. "Please, Mum; we have to go to Uncle Tim's house right now."

Grudgingly her mother had agreed if only to prove Kitty wrong. They drove to Uncle Tim's house to find the police breaking down the door and paramedics waiting to get in.

It turned out Tim's neighbour had heard the crash. He'd looked out of his back bedroom window and had seen Tim's ladder on the ground. Then he had seen Tim on the floor of the conservatory, surrounded by the broken glass of the roof, lying in a pool of blood.

An elderly gentleman, he couldn't hop the back fence to get to Tim, so he had no choice but to call for help and then watch as Tim bled out, alone.

After that, Kitty's parents no longer doubted her abilities. Instead, they blamed her for Tim's death. They treated her as though her vision had made the accident happen. They treated her like she had killed Tim herself. Those final six months, living at home had been unbearable for Kitty. In the end, her parents had been all too happy to sign the release forms when she told them she was enlisting with the Army on her seventeenth birthday.

She'd left a month later and hadn't seen them again after that, not until she saw the vision of her father's death from cancer. She had reached out to her mother then, and once again, she had been blamed. This time for her father's cancer and his death. As if her visions had somehow made him sick and had caused him to die. When she had seen and felt her own mother's death six months later, she made no effort to contact any surviving family members. In fact, she'd heard nothing from anyone for a year until she returned from Iraq to a letter from her parents' solicitor telling them she had inherited their estate.

By that time, she and Jack were trying to get pregnant so that they could have a family of their own. She sold her parent's home and bought her three-bedroomed home in Surrey for her little family to live together instead. She used the rest of her inheritance to set up little nest eggs for the girls after they were born.

Six months after their birth, she had had a vision of an upcoming attack on the Royal Family. She turned to the one person she trusted to believe her, Peter.

She had never seen the vision of her own husband's death, though, and she had often wondered why. In fact, she hadn't had a single vision during her pregnancy with the twins. Was it because of her pregnancy or because of her own grief over Jack's death? She had never been able to figure it out. Certainly, some psychics she had spoken to had told her their visions were more potent than ever during pregnancy. Yet, some had told her they, too, had received nothing during pregnancy. She also knew it wasn't uncommon to stop having visions during times of profound grief.

What if Anthony knew the truth about her, and her mission to rescue the hostages failed? Would the grief be too much to cope with if he blamed her? Would she lose her visions again? Kitty tried to push the thoughts to the back of her mind. She focused on writing out assignments for each person in her team and the police officers who had been drafted in to help with the search. She couldn't think about her feelings for Anthony right now. After all, it was just a silly crush and nothing more. Wasn't it?

Anthony stood in the main school hall as his staff team's sad, desperate, pleading, tear-filled eyes stared back at him. He had just broken the news to his team about the abduction and hostage situation that had unfolded just over an hour ago. All of the students were contained in their classrooms and were being supervised by police officers. The school was quiet. Too quiet.
He knew all of his students knew there was something serious going on, but they didn't know what it was. He would have to call an emergency assembly next to share what he could with them before those who weren't boarding went home for the evening. He didn't want his students to find out what was going on online. It was his job to tell them the truth. But who would he tell?

His school took students from three years old to eighteen years old. He was responsible for children in pre-primary, primary and secondary year groups. At what age should the children in his care have knowledge of this information? Primary was too young, in his opinion, but two of the missing students had sisters in primary year groups. Clare had a daughter in year two. What was he going to tell her about where her mother was?

There were more than a hundred sets of eyes staring at him as he stood at the front of the oak-panelled school hall. He could see how pained and distressed they were, and he had nothing to offer them. He couldn't make it better for any of them. He couldn't tell them that their friends and colleagues would be safe. He couldn't tell them Fitz wasn't being beaten at that very moment. He couldn't promise all ten of the young girls he was responsible for would be going home safely that evening.

He could only tell them one thing. So he did.

"I know that we've all had our misconceptions about Kitty over the years," he told the large group of men and women in front of him. "She fooled us all into believing she was something she's not. However, we all have to accept that her reasons were in the interests of national security."

His colleagues didn't look convinced, and he couldn't blame them for that. It was hard to accept the fact that Kitty had managed to withhold the truth about her identity. It was hard to accept that any of this was real. It was hard to believe that Kitty really was a government agent and not this vulnerable, fragile woman she had convinced them she was.

"The very fact that she was able to keep us all in the dark for so many years proves that she is very good at her job," he continued. "It can't have been easy for her, especially lying to her own children. It is our job now to forgive that and trust that she didn't make it to the rank of General without being very, very good at her job. You've seen her team arriving. You've seen the helicopters on the school field. You've seen how even the police are following her lead. We have to let go of who we all thought she was and trust that the person she really is can save the lives of our missing friends and students."

Anthony couldn't help but wonder if his need to defend Kitty and stress the importance of her role in all of this was misguided. Was he trying to justify his own misconceptions of her? Was he trying to justify his feelings for her? He couldn't even make sense of his feelings for her anymore. Previously, he'd managed to convince himself time and again that he didn't really have any feelings for her at all. That he just felt protective of her because she was a vulnerable, single mother with children in his care.

Yet, she had plagued his dreams night after night for seven years. He'd woken up longing for her more times than he could count. Yet through it all, some part of him disapproved of her. He hated being near her, yet he hated it even more when he saw her walk out of the front doors, not knowing how long it would be until he would next see her. Had he disapproved of her because it was easier than admitting that he had feelings for her?

And what of those feelings now? She was responsible for brings his staff and students home alive. If she failed, would he ever forgive her? If she succeeded, would he finally be able to admit to her how he felt about her? He had no answers and was angry at himself for even thinking of her at a time like this.

He dismissed his staff from the hall and asked those with year seven or above students to return with their tutor groups for an assembly. He also asked to see the three younger students he needed to talk to privately with their teachers. Those were two students he to tell about their missing sisters, and Clare's daughter who had to know that her mummy had been taken by bad men. He needed to focus on that right now. He would deal with his feelings for Kitty later.

Half an hour later, Anthony walked into the meeting room where Kitty and her team had set up their base of operations and stood in the doorway. Kitty saw him and nodded, effectively inviting him into the room. He was grateful to her for allowing his presence in the room and leant against the doorway. All eyes were on Kitty as she stood up in front of a whiteboard. She was about to say something, and he was grateful that she had allowed him in to listen to her speak. He had been sure he would be turned away at the door. Still, he had tried and had been granted access to a top security briefing.
"Right," she called loudly. "Find your seats, and let's have some hush."

Anthony remained in the doorway, watching her intently as everyone else in the room settled down. He was in awe of the way she carried her authority. This was a whole new side of Kitty that he hadn't seen before. He realised her airheaded, whatever, whenever attitude for all these years had been an act. He realised he had judged her based on his own narrow-minded perception of her and not on who she really was. Mind you, he couldn't help that. It seemed she was very good at hiding her true self, which he guessed had been the point. He realised now that she had actually been very, very good at her little act.

"For those of you who don't know, this is Chief Superintendent Peter Lee", Kitty said. She pointed at the slightly greying uniformed police officer, who was leaning back in a plastic school chair.

Anthony nodded politely in his direction. They had met on multiple occasions as he often stopped by to visit Kitty's children on occasions they boarded. He was listed on record as the twins' guardian in the event of Kitty's death. The girls only boarded at school when he had been unavailable to take them into his own home. That had only been the case a few times over the years. Kitty turned and looked at Anthony. For a brief moment, he felt something in the pit of his stomach that he just couldn't place. He tried desperately to ignore that all too familiar spark of electricity he felt whenever their eyes met.

"And this, ladies and gentlemen, is Anthony Richmond. He is the school's headteacher. I have granted him access to this meeting as what happens here directly impacts him, his staff and most importantly, his students."

"Excuse me, General," a hand shot up at the back of the room.

"Yes, Sergeant," she answered as she turned to face the man at the back of the room who was wearing an Army uniform and had cropped blonde hair.

"I mean no disrespect to the headteacher, but should he really be in this briefing? How well do we know him, and can we be sure we can trust him?"

"I've trusted him every day for seven years with the lives of my children," Kitty responded. "In all that time, he has never once let me down or caused me any reason to doubt his integrity."

"No offence General," the Sergeant continued, "but that is slightly different."

"No, Christopher, it's not," Kitty sighed impatiently. "My kids are here because of the dangers of my job. They are here because this man runs an institution that protects the children of some very influential people. And quite frankly, if I can trust Mr Richmond with the lives of my children, I can trust him with anything."

Oh boy. Anthony's heart swelled in his chest. Even at the darkest of times, Kitty was able to make him feel something other than the sickening fear that had been ripping him apart for the past hour. He wasn't sure if she really meant it or if it was another one of her award-worthy acts, but he let the words wash over him, and he let himself take a few moments of comfort from them. Looking at her, he mouthed silently, "Thank you."

She smiled softly and mouthed back, "You're welcome."

For a moment, they just held each other's gaze, and for Anthony at that moment, he felt nothing but her warmth circling his heart. He wasn't sure how long they stared at each other, but the sound of the Chief Superintendent clearing his throat caused them both to snap their gazes away.

"This is what we know so far," Kitty continued as if the moment hadn't phased her at all. "At approximately thirteen forty hours, six S.W.O terrorists took these thirteen people hostage at gunpoint." She pointed at the list of names and faces she had previously stuck to the whiteboard. Anthony looked at them, and all over again, a wave of nausea washed over him. It was a harsh reminder as to why he was even in the meeting in the first place.

"Each of the hostages was bound, gagged and covered with a black hood. The three staff members were also struck with a rounders bat. We know the exact location of where they were when they were taken. What we don't know is where they are now, whether or not they have changed vehicles. We don't whether anyone needs medical attention or exactly who these S.W.O terrorists are and what they want. We believe Mr Fitzwilliams will require medical attention soon if he doesn't already. There was also no blood at the scene to track any of the hostages with."

Blood? Anthony was confused and relieved in equal measure. He was thankful that there had been no evidence of any serious injuries at the scene but had no idea how blood would have helped her to track the hostages. He wanted to raise his hand like one of his students and ask the question, but he didn't feel qualified to interrupt Kitty.

"Are we happy saying these are definitely S.W.O terrorists at this point, General?" someone asked.

"Yes, absolutely," Kitty confirmed. "We know from the language they used, their particular hatred of Mr Fitzwilliams and their general behaviour that these men are S.W.O terrorists. There is no doubt in my mind whatsoever that we are dealing with S.W.O. We'd heard chatter that they were planning something. Unfortunately, our undercover operative hadn't been able to get high enough in the ranks to find out exactly what and when.

Anthony watched Kitty as she stopped to take a breath. It seemed she could spill out multiple sentences without needing to breathe in between for quite a while. *She'd make a good teacher*, he mused.

Again he stared at her, still completely surprised by this side of her that he was seeing him for the first time. She was amazing.

Kitty must have felt his eyes on her as she looked back at him, and her gaze softened. They held each other's gazes, and for a brief moment, he could feel no one in the room but her. Then her eyes grew sharp, and she shook her head and turned away. All too soon, Anthony was once again facing the reality of the situation around him.

"Liaisons for each department will be as follows," Kitty continued. "For the police force, it'll be Chief Superintendent Lee. For my office, it'll be Lieutenant Kate Mitchell. For MI5, it'll be Simon Clarkson. For the school, it'll be Mr Richmond. All liaisons will report directly to me. At this stage, I will not be heading into the field. I know this school, I know the staff, and I know the students. My own children are also here right now, so my role will be to support the school in any way I can and coordinate things from here. Any questions?"

Anthony watched as everyone sat in silence, some of the people in the room shaking their heads.

"Good," Kitty continued. "In that case, I'll hand over to the other Kathryn, who will hand out assignments."

Kate stood up and took the floor as Kitty headed toward the door. Anthony watched her approach, and his breath caught as she made eye contact with him.

"Let's take a walk," she said to him as she headed out of the room.

Anthony said nothing. He knew she didn't need him to. He simply followed her out of the room as she led the way to his office.

Six

"That can't happen again," Kitty said firmly as she opened the door to Anthony's office. She walked in ahead of him as if she owned the space and stopped in the middle of the room before turning to face Anthony. At six foot four inches, he towered above her, so she pushed her shoulders back and stood as tall as she could. She needed to find her power. It wasn't something she usually had any problem with unless she was with Anthony. She felt powerless around him, and she shouldn't afford to let that happen today.

"What can't happen again?" Anthony asked. "And please, do come in," he added sarcastically, closing the door behind them.

"That," she snapped as she mentally reminded herself that she was strong and she was in control this time. "In there. You looking at me as if I was the only person in the room or as if you were finally just seeing me for the first time."

"Finally?" Anthony asked.

Crap! She hadn't meant to say that. She didn't want to give anything away about her feelings or how vulnerable she felt around him. She would have to do better if she was going to at least pretend to feel strong around him this time.

"You know what I mean," Kitty said as calmly as she could with a dismissive wave of her manicured hand.

It wasn't that Anthony was controlling or belittling toward her; nothing could be further from the truth. It was her own feelings for him that took her hostage whenever he was around. Her dirty little crush. The way just being around him made her heart beat faster, and her resolve feel weaker. She was under his spell, and no matter how much she tried to deny it, she knew it was true. This was a different kind of witchcraft, and it felt like a curse.

"I know I've never known you to say something you don't mean," Anthony said as he leant against the cream coloured wall near the closed office door and stared at her.

Kitty felt flustered. More than that, though, she felt angry, and she felt afraid.

"Look, Anthony," she said hotly. "You can't have a go at me for trying to flirt with you when I wasn't, and then an hour later, stand there and look at me like you want to stick your fucking tongue down my fucking throat."

She knew she was overacting. She knew she was probably being unfair. She and Anthony had flirted harmlessly before, and to her, his part had always just seemed meaningless. She'd just assumed he was like that with everyone. The charming headteacher knew how to win over the mums in school to get them on side. This time though, it had felt different. It was as though something had shifted between them, and it felt like so much more than the innocent flirty techniques he'd used in the past to get her to encourage her kids to join the school choir.

"I did no such thing," Anthony barked. "I looked at you as someone who was grateful for your kind words. Especially, when for the first time in longer than I can remember, I have zero control of what is going on around me. I looked at you with gratitude and respect and maybe just a hint of friendship, but I should have known your speech was just another one of your little acts."

"What the hell does that-" But she stopped.

Her breath caught in her throat, and she was no longer present in the room. She was no longer herself at all. She was a tall, well-built, battered and bruised black man with a gun to his head and a rounders bat hurled into his abdomen at full force. She was Fitz, and she was in agony, and she was terrified.

Anthony looked at Kitty. Something wasn't right. Her eyes had glazed over, and she was swooning. He shot across the room and was by her side within three seconds.

"Kitty," he said. "Kitty." His voice was more urgent the second time as he wrapped an arm around her waist and held onto her firmly. Was she going to pass out? She was pale, and beads of sweat were starting to form on her temples. She looked like she was going to be sick, but he didn't dare let go of her to grab the little waste bin that sat next to the mahogany table in the corner of his office. Instead, he gently used his free hand to brush the thick chocolate brown curls that had escaped from her ponytail, away from her face, so that if she did throw up, at least she wouldn't get it in her hair. He felt her legs buckle, and they gave way. He took her bodyweight and gently eased her down to the floor, taking himself down with her and cradling her against his chest, and holding two strong, supportive arms around her. If she was sick now, he would be covered in it, but he didn't care. Something about what was happening filled him with the urge to protect her, and he wanted to hold her close to him and never let go.

"Kitty," he said one more time as he gently lifted a hand to stroke her face.

How was it in the space of a minute this beautiful, brave woman had gone from looking so strong to so weak? She had become the living embodiment of what he was feeling. Was she actually battling with some untold illness after all? Had their argument induced the loss of consciousness? Had he done this to her? He couldn't stand the thought that he had somehow made her ill, so he pushed it to the back of his mind and decided he would try one more time to rouse her before he would have to call for help. "Kitty. Kitty, can you hear me?"

She stirred slowly. She began to tremble and buried her head in his chest, wrapping her arm around his neck to pull him closer. Something about the way she pulled him to her made his heart lurch. It wasn't a move of passion. It was a move of pure fear and the need to feel comforted and protected. He'd seen it before when young children had come in for their first day at school and clung to their mothers like she was their lifeline. Kitty was now shaking and sobbing fiercely. Something had frightened her, but what?

What had happened between them arguing and now to make her so terrified? He knew by the way she was clinging so tightly to him that it wasn't him she was scared of, and he knew whatever it was, it was genuine. This definitely wasn't an act of any sort. No one could seem this terrified, and it not be real. Not letting go of Kitty once, he shifted position and kicked off his black leather loafers. He shuffled back along the hardwood floor until his back was pressed against the wall. He pulled Kitty onto his lap and cradled her in his arms.

"Kate," Kitty choked finally. "Get Kate." Anthony was relieved to finally hear Kitty's voice, even though those few short words sounded so broken. Not wanting to let her go or leave her in this state, he did the only thing he could think of. He pulled his mobile phone from his pocket and called the school's main switchboard number.

He didn't recognise the voice of the man who answered the phone. That was hardly a surprise given that Kitty's team had seized control of the school's phone lines.

"This is Anthony Richmond. I need to see Lieutenant Mitchell in my office urgently."

He clicked off, put his phone on the floor and turned his attention back to Kitty. Still keeping one arm firmly around her, he brought his other hand up to her head and began to stroke her soft brown curls. He pressed his lips to her head and began to whisper soothing words to her, in between placing gentle kisses on her forehead. "It's O.K. Kitty," he whispered. "I've got you. You're safe." He followed that with, "Shh baby, it's alright, you're safe. I've got you, baby. I'm not going to let you go."

Anthony felt every word and each kiss deeply as they left his mouth. He wanted to pull back and ponder what his actions meant, but he didn't get the chance. The door to his office bust in, and Kate Mitchell rushed in.

"What the hell happened?" She demanded, dropping to her knees in front of where Anthony was cradling a still sobbing Kitty.

"I have no idea," He admitted. "One minute we were yelling at each other, and the next Kitty stopped mid-sentence. Her eyes glazed over, and she lost consciousness."

"Fuck," Kate shot. "How long was she out?"

"A few minutes maybe less," he said. "Do you know what's wrong with her?"

"She's too close to this case," Kate said. "It's causing her visions to hit her pretty hard."

"I'm sorry?" Anthony asked, hoping he didn't look our sound as dumbfounded as he felt. "Did you just say visions?"

"The General is a psychic," Kate said as casually as if she just told him it was raining outside.

"The hell she is," Anthony said hotly. "There's no such thing."

"No?" Kate asked. "How exactly do you think she knew all those details of the kidnapping?"

"Fitz," Kitty whispered, interrupting.

"What about him?" Anthony asked before Kate could.

"He was able to break the ties on his wrists and pulled the hood off. They're in a factory. A disused one. It stinks of fish."

"That's great, Kitty," Kate said. "What else did you see?"

Anthony felt Kitty's grip tighten around his neck and her body pull closer to his before she answered. He held her tighter, unwilling to let her go while she was in this state.

"They caught him'" she choked. "He made them angry. They were shouting and waving their guns around. They pulled the hood back over his face, and he could hear the girls and women screaming as they dragged him from the room. He was so scared. Not for himself but for what they might do to the females. They took the hood back off and held a gun to his head while beating him with the rounders bat. Then they hit him over the head with the butt of the rifle, and he lost consciousness."

Kitty returned to sobbing into Anthony's chest.

Anthony looked at Kate. "Is that why Kitty lost consciousness? Because Fitz did?"

"Yes," Kate confirmed. "Especially if the vision was real-time. Those are the visions that hit her the hardest, and as I said, she's very close to this case. Take care of her. Let her rest and stay with her until she feels better."

"What do I do?" he asked. He had never cared for someone who was apparently recovering from a psychic vision before. Up until a minute ago, he was sure there was no such thing. Now he didn't know what to think, but he knew that Kitty believed they were real and she needed him. Anthony felt Kate's knowing gaze settling over him. "Just keep doing the things you were doing when I came in. I need to report this information to the team and start looking for warehouses connected to fish."

"It's not a lot to go on," he sighed.

"I've worked with less and had good results," Kate assured him. "I'll send a medic in to check on her shortly, but let her calm down a little first. She's not in any danger, she's just emotionally beaten, but this is Kitty. She'll bounce right back after some rest and will be ready to kick some arse."

"That I do believe," Anthony said as he smiled slightly.

"You know our girl," Kate said as she got to her feet and hurried from the room, closing the door behind her.

"I thought I did," Anthony said to himself quietly. He shifted slightly and lifted Kitty into his arms. His heart was pounding in his chest as he carefully manoeuvred himself into a standing position and carried her over to the large brown leather sofa in his office. Leaning forward, he carefully laid down on the sofa under his office window and stepped back. He'd been terrified of dropping her while trying to get up from the floor without being able to use his arms. An instant wave of relief had washed over him the moment he had safely lowered her onto the leather. "Please don't leave me," Kitty whispered, reaching out a hand. "It's so dark."

Anthony crouched down in front of Kitty, took her outstretched hand in his and stroked her hair with his other hand. She looked exhausted, and she looked broken. It tore him apart to see her so fragile.

He'd never seen Kitty look so weak and vulnerable before, and it hurt him to see it now. He loved her strength and fiery spirit, but he could see no fire in those hazel eyes now. The Kitty he knew was gone. He wasn't sure she had ever really existed. Was the Kitty he knew just a charade? Had he had feelings for someone who wasn't even real for the past seven years if that was true? He'd told himself that what he was feeling hadn't been real, yet it had been enough to keep him from forming any other sort of romantic attachment.

He'd tried to date. Plenty of women had been interested. Yet he'd never been able to get past the first two or three dates with someone as deep down he had always been drawn to this one woman. Certainly none of them had made it into his bed. Now he was realising, all of that may have been a lie and he could have wasted years of his life alone, for nothing.

"I'm not leaving you," he whispered. "I'm just letting you rest. When you feel better, we'll talk about everything."

"What's the point?" Kitty sighed. "You said you don't believe in psychics."

"I didn't believe," he agreed. "Now, I'm not so sure."

"Why?" Kitty asked.

"Because I'm a man of science," Anthony said simply.

"No, I mean, why aren't you so sure now?"

Anthony stood, walked to his desk and grabbed one of the brown leather tub chairs from in front of it. He carried it over to where Kitty lay on the sofa and set it down in front of her.

"There's no way you could have made up being that distressed," he said as he sat in the chair. "And besides, I get the feeling this isn't the first time Kate has found answers with one of your visions."

"And so you accepted it, just like that?" Kitty asked.

Anthony sighed. Had he actually accepted it, or was it just something he was feeling in the moment? The scientist in him was cringing at the mere thought of accepting that someone could possess psychic powers. Yet something in his gut told him Kitty wasn't making this up.

"Did you mean what you said about trusting me?" He asked, answering her question with a question.

Kitty nodded.

"Then trust that I trust you," he said. "You say you receive visions, and until I have proof to the contrary, I will trust that what you say is true." Of course, that didn't mean he wouldn't look for evidence of the truth either way. He would. He needed to know that she wasn't a charlatan or, worse, insane. Especially now that the lives of thirteen people were hanging in the balance. His people.

"Thank you," Kitty whispered as a long, sleepy yawn escaped her.

"Close your eyes," Anthony told her.

"I can't," she said as she tried to sit up. "I need to get back out there. I need to get to work."

"You need to rest," he said as he gently placed a hand on her shoulder to keep her from moving. "Your team knows what they are doing. They will come for you when they need you."

"Will you stay with me?" She asked, closing her eyes.

"I need to go and deal with parents and students," he said. "Those students who can be collected are being picked up at four o'clock. I need to check that the escorts you've arranged are ready and that we can safely remove as many students as possible from site. I also need to see that everyone is signed out to the correct parent or guardian."

And if he was honest with himself, Anthony needed to get away from Kitty for a while. She was clouding is ability to focus. She was teasing his senses, and the way she had felt in his arms had been torture for him. He needed to get back out there and do his job, even if he couldn't stand the thought of walking out the door and leaving Kitty behind. How had things shifted between them so quickly?

"Yes," Kitty agreed. "You must do that. Just send someone to wake me in half an hour, please. I honestly don't usually get like this after visions, but this one hit me pretty hard."

"It's personal this time," Anthony said, taking Kitty's hand in his. "You know these people. Your children know them. And I don't really know what I'm talking about here, but is it possible you're feeling the after-effects of Fitz's head injury?"

"It's entirely possible," Kitty said. "They hit him pretty hard."

She tried to suppress a shudder, but Anthony didn't miss it. He saw her body tense, and her hand gripped his just a little tighter.

"Sleep now," he commanded. "I'll come back for you as soon as I have safely evacuated as many students as possible."

He stood and strode across the room and shoved his feet back into his shoes. He went to leave, but he turned around for one last look at Kitty as he opened the door. He needed to get his head in the game and focus on the tasks ahead. But as he looked at her, knowing he was going to leave her, his heart lurched. He'd made a huge mistake letting her in after resisting her for so many years, and he knew he would never be able to shut her out again.

Seven

Kitty awoke to the sound of familiar chit-chat. She opened her eyes as saw her two teenage daughters peering over her.

"Mr Richmond said we could wake you," Ivy said.

So, Anthony had sent her daughters to wake her rather than coming back himself. Clearly, he was avoiding her, but why? Had things changed that much between them? Was he angry at her, or did he think she was some sort of freak who claimed to have psychic powers?

"He said you suddenly felt unwell and needed to sleep," Rosie added.

"But then he said it was time to wake you and asked us if we would do it," Ivy told Kitty, who was alternating between rubbing her eyes and blinking.

Oh, he was definitely avoiding her. He'd sent Ivy and Rosie to wake her so he didn't have to see her or be alone with her. Kitty had been sure he wouldn't be able to handle the truth about her. Clearly, she was right. She sat up and smiled at her daughters, not wanting to give them any hint that anything was wrong.

"What time is it?" she asked, sitting up slowly.

"It's a little after 5pm," Rosie said. "Sir told us to let you sleep until five and then wake you."

"Shit," Kitty said, scrambling to her feet.

"Mother!" Rosie gasped.

Kitty had sworn in front of her daughters before but never in their headteacher's office. Mind you, she had never napped in his office before today either. It really was a day of firsts.

"I'm going to pick you both up some things from home," Kitty said, leaning in to kiss both of her daughters atop their heads in turn. "We're going to be staying here until this situation is dealt with."

"You can't leave Mum," Ivy said.

"Why?" Kitty asked softly as she looked down at her two precious daughters. "Did something else happen? Are you two O.K?"

"We're fine, Mum," Ivy said.

"Uncle Pete said you aren't allowed to leave until you've seen the doctor," Rosie said as she shrugged her shoulders.

Crap! She knew she could argue about seeing the doctor, but she also knew he could relieve her of her command if she didn't stay and see him. There was no messing around when it came to the health of her team, particularly those with supernatural abilities. She would have to wait for the doctor and jump through as many hoops as needed if she was going to get back to work.

"Fine," she said finally. "And then I will go home and get us some things. You'll both have to stay here until this is all sorted and we know things are safe."

The girls didn't argue; they just nodded. Her kids weren't stupid. They knew she would keep them here with all of the armed police and soldiers. She knew they wouldn't like it, but she knew they wouldn't resist either.

"Students are going to be moved into the main hall," she told her daughters. "We have the Army bringing in camp beds and sleeping bags."

"Oh, the rich kids are going to love that," Ivy teased.

"They'll have to suck it up, right, Mum?" Rosie said.

"You bet they will," Kitty said. "It's safer if we can keep you all together with a lot of security rather than dotted around in different dorms with less security. Just promise me you won't say a word about me to any of the other girls."

"We promise," they said together.

"One of these days," she told her daughters. "You're going to have to tell me how you do that."

"You wouldn't believe us if we did," Ivy said.

"Oh, I think you'll find I would," Kitty said as she leant forward to kiss her daughters before they were interrupted by a knock on the door.

"What's the deal with you and Kitty anyway?" Anthony sat forward in his seat and stared at Kate. She wasn't shy about saying what was on her mind.

"Deal?" he asked as casually as he could. "There is no deal. I'm the headteacher, and she's a parent."

"Right," Kate said.

Anthony turned his attention to the display board on the wall in front of him. He'd looked at this board hundreds of times over the years but never so intently. He took in every last detail of the reception class artwork that was on display. Funny round blobs with arms, legs, wonky eyes and lopsided smiles greeted him. One of them had his name written underneath it in the reception teacher's handwriting. This was a collection of drawings the kids had made of teachers in the school.

"So those looks between you earlier were nothing then?" Kate pressed after a few moments.

Anthony sighed. She clearly wasn't going to let this one go.

"I guess we're sort of friends," he shrugged. "Her children have been here for a long time. Parents and staff get to know each other over time, and sometimes friendships begin to form."

"Right," Kate said. "Friends."

Anthony stared at the drawing of himself. His blob-shaped body was long and narrow. He looked like a pea pod. Clearly, whoever drew this had noticed that he was tall and athletic, and he appreciated their observation skills. In the next drawing, poor pregnant Mrs Carter looked like a beach ball who had become tangled up in seaweed. Not very flattering, given that she was only sporting a neat little baby bump in reality. He looked from the wall to Kate, who was alternating between working on the two laptops in front of her. Each of them sat atop heavy-duty metallic briefcases that he was sure were made of Kevlar. He sat quietly and watched her for a moment until she looked up at him.

"That's it," she said, placing her hands palms down on the table.

"That's what?" Anthony asked, unsure of what was going on. Had he offended her or annoyed her in some way?

"We both know you're not just sitting here for the fun of it," Kate said. "So what is it you've been sat here for the past ten minutes trying to figure out how to ask me, Mr Richmond?"

Anthony sighed. She was right. He had wanted to ask her something, but he wasn't sure how to ask it without sounding like a complete moron, and he wasn't sure he was going to like the answer either.

"Just spit it out, Teach," Kate insisted. "You'll feel better after."

"Kitty trusts me, right?" Anthony asked. "With this case, I mean."

"She trusts you," Kate confirmed.

"And you?" He asked.

"As my boss," Kate started. "I trust Kitty's judgement, and if she trusts you, I trust you. But as my dear friend, I'm not sure I trust you with her heart."

That seemed fair, Anthony mused. He wasn't sure he trusted himself with Kitty's heart either. He knew he would never intentionally hurt her, but he didn't know what he felt or if it was even real. He needed to remember that before allowing himself to get any closer to Kitty. He could have his own heart ripped out, but he didn't want to do anything to damage hers.

"So, could I please ask you a question then?" Anthony asked, deciding not to respond to the bit about Kitty's heart until he was sure of what his own heart wanted.

"If it's about Kitty, I think you should ask her yourself," Kate said.

Anthony stood, clasped his hands behind his lower back and began to pace the room. He needed to ask his question, but he still wasn't sure he wouldn't sound like an idiot. Finally, after walking the length of the room twice, he turned back to Kate.

"I want to ask about something Kitty said at the briefing," he said as he unclasped his hands. He rested them on the back of the grey plastic chair he had been sitting on moments earlier. "About blood."

"Shoot," Kate said.

Her eyes were back on her laptop screen, and Anthony wasn't sure if he should just leave her to her work. He didn't want to disturb her or prevent her from focusing on finding his missing staff and students. Yet, he really felt like he had missed something important at the meeting, and he needed to ask about it so he could get a better idea of how blood could have been used to track the hostages if there had been any.

"You can ask," Kate said, briefly glancing up from her screen. "I promise, I can do what I'm doing here and talk to you at the same time. If there is something about the investigation that is bothering you, it's better to talk about it."

Talk about a woman's intuition, Anthony thought. It was as though she knew exactly what he had been thinking. He decided to just ask the question and get it over with. He didn't want to take up too much more of Kate's time when she was trying to track possible locations the hostages might be in and relay that to ground troops. Or at least that was how she had described it to him when he had first popped in to see her after he'd finished safely dismissing students.

"Kitty said that had there have been blood at the scene, it could have been used to help track the hostages," he said as he began to build up to his question. "I was wondering, exactly how would that have worked? It's not like they would have left a trail of droplets from the minibus to wherever they went, so how would you have been able to track the hostages that way?"

"A blood calling blood spell," Kate shrugged.

"A what?" Anthony asked.

Surely he didn't hear that correctly. First psychic visions and now spells using human blood. This was starting to feel more like a cult than a government organisation.

"It's quite simple," Kate told him, glancing up from her laptop once more. "If we have enough fresh blood, we can use it to track the host body it came from. The spell itself is quite easy, but anything outside a mile radius, and it requires an entire coven to perform."

"This can't be real," Anthony said as he released the back of the chair and resumed pacing the length of the room. By the time this was over, he was sure he would wear holes in the grey carpet with his loafers.

"What can't be real?" Kate asked as she also stood.

"Witchcraft, psychic powers, blood spells. There's no scientific basis for any of this."

Anthony felt sick. He was trusting the safe return of his staff and students to a group of deluded, crazy people. There was no way this stuff was actually real. Was Kitty's team even real, or was this all some sort of elaborate scam?

Kate cleared her throat, and Anthony stopped pacing and looked at her.

She stepped back from the table and held her arms out by her side, each one about a foot away from her body, palms facing forward.

Anthony watched her but said nothing. What was this? Was she going to start chanting in some ancient language and then profess to have a psychic message from beyond the other side? As he watched and waited, though, Kate said nothing. He kept waiting for the weird chanting to begin and the inevitable rolling on the eyes and panting that would follow, coupled with the announcement that a message was coming through from his grandmother. What he saw, though, was something he could never have imagined was possible in reality.

Kate gently lifted off the ground and levitated about two feet above the grey carpeted floor. She just floated there in mid-air with a huge grin on her face as she moved her arms until her hands were resting on her hips.

He stepped back in surprise, unable to form any words, unable to get any words out of his gaped open mouth at all. He just stood there trying to work out what the hell was going on. How she was pulling off such an elaborate trick. He looked from Kate to the whitewashed high ceiling in the room and back to Kate again.

"That's… That's not possible," Anthony finally managed to stammer.

He felt a slight sense of panic as Kate lifted herself higher until she glided toward him above the table.

"Want to check for wires?" she asked as she hovered over the table.

Anthony didn't move. For the first time in his life, he was frozen on the spot. Unable to speak, unable to take a step forward. He just stood there, too stunned to do anything.

Kate laughed and moved her arms until they were out in front of her just enough that they were still bent at the elbows. She balled her hands into fists, her inner wrists facing up toward the ceiling. Very quickly, she brought her arms together until the sides of her two fists smacked together. As she pulled them away from each other just as fast, she opened her hands and two fireballs formed in her palms.

As flames floated neatly in the palms of Kate's hands, Anthony finally moved. He shot across the room and grabbed the red fire extinguisher that was mounted to the wall. As he turned back, Kate was still hovering with the fireballs floating about an inch above her hands. Her head was tilted back, and she was roaring with laughter.

Before he had even pulled the pin from the fire extinguisher, Kate clapped her hands together, and the flames disappeared.

"What the fuck?" Anthony gasped as he stood there holding the fire extinguisher, feeling like a bit of an idiot.

Kate lowered herself until she was standing on the table.

"Don't feel bad," a voice came from behind him. Anthony turned around to see Chief Superintendent Peter Lee standing in the doorway.

"The first time I saw Kate do this, I ran and ducked for cover," Peter chuckled. "At least you had the sense to run for a fire extinguisher."

Anthony dumped the extinguisher on the floor by his feet. Peter entered the room and moved over to the table, holding a hand out for Kate. Kate took it and hopped down from the table.

Anthony glared at both of them.

"I suppose you two think this is hilarious?" he asked, hearing the frustrated tone in his own voice.

"A little," Peter admitted. "But only because I've been where you are."

"I'm sorry," Kate said, the smile disappearing from her face. "There was no gentle way to do that. Not today. I could see you were starting to doubt our ability to find and rescue your missing staff and kids. You needed to understand exactly what it is we're capable of. Now I need you to trust us to get them home, the way we're now trusting you with our secret."

Anthony thought about this for a moment. What Kate had just shown him was enough to bring witch trials back to the U.K. Yet, she had trusted him enough to show him the truth about who she really was. This was the power she had to get his people home safely.

He couldn't un-see what he had just seen. He needed to trust her now. He needed to trust Kitty too.

"So," he said finally, as he sat down in one of the plastic chairs at the table. "Magic is real."

"Yep, Kitty said, as she and Peter also sat.

"What else do I need to know?" He asked. "What about Kitty? Can she bang her fists together and launch fire from her hands?"

"The fire thing is specific to me," Kate said. "Kitty has a different skill set."

"And she packs a pretty mean punch," Peter added as he leant back in his chair.

"You know," Kate said. "Kitty would have told you all of this when she was ready. It's just that she's been hurt a lot in the past, and so now she doesn't tell anyone she has supernatural abilities until she can be sure of how they're going to react."

"You had no problem telling me, and we've only just met," Anthony reminded Kate.

"Exactly," Kate said. "If you'd lost your shit, I wouldn't have cared. It wouldn't have hurt me. But you and Kitty are close. Closer than either of you are willing to admit."

"Look, I care for Kitty the same way I care for all of the parents in this school," Anthony said. Yet he knew as he said it he was lying not only to those in the room but also to himself.

"You're sat in a room with two trained observers," Peter reminded him. "I'll bet anything that when Kitty hauled you out of this room earlier, she gave you a right telling off about the lovey-dovey looks you were giving each other."

"How did you know?" Anthony asked.

"Because Kitty knows that everyone in the room would have noticed that, and she would have been embarrassed about it," Kate said, shrugging. "She doesn't like to show any sort of vulnerability. She certainly doesn't want her team thinking she's compromised because she's banging the headteacher."

"Kitty and I are not having sex," Anthony snapped as he stood up from his chair once more.

"We know," Kate said.

"Trust me," Peter added. "If Kitty was getting some action, she wouldn't be anywhere near as tightly wound as she is now. She'd be a lot less stressed and better able to focus if she had a good shag."

"So you think I should have sex with her so she'll feel better?" Anthony asked. "Is that how Kitty operates? She screws whichever guy is nearest and most convenient to make her better at her job."

He had resumed his pacing of the room. This time his arms were folded across his chest as if he was trying to protect his heart.

"What?" Kate gasped. "No, of course not. Kitty's not been involved with anyone in years."

"We've not seen her this stressed in years either," Peter admitted.

"We just think some feel-good hormones will give her a sense of calm and clarity," Kate said.

"And you want me to give that to her?" Anthony shot. "I don't have sex with the mothers at my school."

"No," Kate sighed. "You just fall in love with them and then torture yourself on your inability to follow through."

"How fucking dare you?"

Anthony was furious. No one had ever dared to talk to him in this manner before. No one had ever accused him of being emotionally impotent. No one had ever told him who he should be having sex with. He'd dreamed of making love to Kitty more times than he could count, but he wasn't prepared to risk his career to take advantage of a vulnerable parent just to satisfy his own needs. He would never hurt Kitty like that. Kitty wasn't a vulnerable parent, though. That had all been an act. Kitty was a strong Army General with supernatural abilities and was probably stronger than he was. She wasn't weak, vulnerable or fragile. She was amazing, and he was only now beginning to realise just how amazing she really was.

Did this change things? He knew Kitty had feelings for him or was at least attracted to him. She wasn't just a school parent anymore. She was a General in the Army and was heading up a special task force in his school. Everything had changed. Could the nature of their relationship also change now that the truth had been revealed? He needed to know.

Without saying another word to either Peter or Kate, Anthony turned and marched right out of the room.

Eight

Kitty had seen the Army doctor and had received the all-clear to return to work. She left Anthony's office with only one thing on her mind, tracking down the missing hostages and rescuing them. It was the only thing she was thinking about as she walked quickly down the corridor. That changed, though, when she turned a corner and bumped right into Anthony.

"You were supposed to wake me," she scolded. She went from focused to pissed off in the space of a second.

Anthony stepped back by four paces. He looked startled, but more than that, he looked upset, and Kitty wanted to know why.

"What's happened?" she demanded.

"What? Oh nothing," he shrugged. "The doctor said you needed to rest for a while longer, and I wasn't about to argue with him."

"Are you alright?" she asked as she looked at him closely. Something had distressed him, and she needed to know what it was.

"I'm fine," Anthony told her. "I've just come from Kate. There's nothing new to report, and I guess I am just feeling worried and impatient."

"I get that," Kitty said. "These things take a lot longer in real life than they do in the movies. We might not find them before tomorrow."

Kitty decided that honesty was the best policy. She needed to manage Anthony's expectations.

"You can't hurry things along?" he asked. "Not even with all of your superpowers?"

"Oh," Kitty said. "I'm guessing Kate gave you a demonstration."

That must be why he looked so worked up and upset. He'd discovered the truth, and he wasn't handling it very well.

"She did," he admitted. "Your friend Peter thought it was hilarious, by the way."

"He didn't think it was so funny when Kate did it to him," Kitty said, a slight smile playing on her lips. "I thought he was going to have a heart attack."

"I almost soaked Kate with a fire extinguisher," Anthony shrugged.

"Well, I'm sorry I missed that," Kitty told him. "There would have been nothing for you to miss if you had just told me the truth from the start," Anthony shot. "I could have heard all of this from you. You said you trusted me, but you never trusted me to deal with the truth. You doubted my ability to accept the real you."

"To be fair," Kitty said. "You don't look like you're handling it too well now."

"I'm not upset about learning you're some supernatural goddess," Anthony said as he leant against a white support pillar in the middle of the corridor. "I'm upset that you didn't trust me enough to tell me about all of this yourself. I thought…"

When he didn't finish the sentence, Kitty sought to find out what Anthony had been about to say. "You thought what?" She asked gently.

"I thought you trusted me," he said.

Now she understood. Anthony was upset because he thought there was something between them. This wasn't just a trust thing; this was about the connection between them that was suddenly growing much faster than it had in the seven years they had known each other. The pained look on his face spoke volumes. He wasn't sure if those little moments of eye contact, smiles and the odd flirty comments they had shared over the years had been real. The truth was, neither did she.

She had spent years lying to him about who she really was, yet today with each piece of the truth he was presented with, he had moved closer to her rather than pulling away. The looks that passed between them had grown more intense, and he had held her in his arms, kissing her head and calling her baby as he'd soothed her earlier. He didn't just fancy her; he had feelings for her.

"Look," she said as she stepped forward and gently tugged his arm until he stood up straight again. She pulled him into an empty classroom and closed the door. She looked around the room at the displays on the walls. Maths. Her least favourite subject.

"You know, and I know that something is going on here," she told him as she perched on one of the blue twin space classroom tables.

"Going on?" he asked.

She knew he would play dumb. She'd spent a lot of time with him in an official capacity over the years, and he'd always played his cards pretty close to his chest. She wasn't expecting that to change now.

"With us, she said. "Something is going on with us."

"I don't know what you are talking about, Kitty," Anthony told her.

He didn't move from the spot he had chosen to stand in upon entering the room. He was right by the closed door, and Kitty wasn't sure if it was because he was too stubborn to move or if it was because he was getting ready to bolt at any minute.

"Oh please," Kitty rolled her eyes. "I was crying, Anthony, not dead. I heard you. I heard every word. I heard your sharp intake of breath when I pulled you closer, felt you kiss my head more than once. I heard the affection in your voice as you soothed me."

"I was trying to comfort you," he insisted. "I had no idea what was going on."

"Fuck my life," Kitty groaned. "You are a bloody terrible liar."

Kitty saw Anthony's shoulders stiffen but just blinked at her without saying a word. He looked shocked. Clearly, he wasn't used to parents talking to him like this. Kitty opted to take his silence as an invitation to continue.

"The truth is, we've both felt a spark for years. It's why you've always looked down on me. You couldn't believe you were attracted to some deadbeat single mum. As for me, I couldn't believe I was attracted to such a stuck up snob."

"Stuck up snob," Anthony repeated. "You think I'm a stuck up snob?"

"Yes," she said, smirking. "But that's not the point."

"What is the point exactly, Kitty?" Anthony asked impatiently. "Because I have work to do, and so do you."

"The point is, I can't get distracted and risk lives by getting involved in a romantic entanglement just to satisfy some desperate need I might have to see what you're like in bed. We can go no further."

"Desperate need?" Anthony questioned.

"More like a strange curiosity," Kitty corrected herself.

"You said desperate need," he reminded her. "You can't take that back."

Kitty felt her face grow hot. Then her neck. From there, the heat spread through her entire body like a wildfire. She stood and manoeuvred around the table. She stepped back and then stepped back some more until she was up against the wall and could go no further. The way Anthony was looking at her made her tingle in her most intimate place, but she needed to keep her distance. She needed to keep her composure. She needed to keep her focus.

Finally, he moved and took a step toward her. The fierce, hungry desire in his silver-grey eyes made her heart race and her knees go weak. She had to reach out and clutch onto a nearby filing cabinet to steady herself. He wanted her as much as she wanted him, and she wasn't sure she had the strength to resist him if he tried to kiss her. She'd burned for him for far too long.

He stepped closer to her until he was barely an arm's length away from her. She put out a hand to stop him but made no real effort to resist his advances as he stepped forward again until her hand settled against his chest. *Fuck*, his heart was pounding as much as hers was.

"No," she said firmly, making a feeble attempt to push him away from her. "I mean it, we can't do this."

Her voice trembled with a mixture of fear and excitement. She wanted this. She needed this. Yet, at the same time, she knew if they did this now, things could get messy and awkward. In her head, she knew now wasn't the time, but the rest of her body was screaming for him.

"Kitty." He said her name in a low, desperate plea. He needed her as much as she needed him.

"Fuck," she gasped as she grabbed him by the front of his suit jacket and pulled him toward her. His mouth found hers with such force she bucked against him. He responded by pressing her into the wall with the full force of his pelvis. She felt his long, hard erection against her and responded by opening her mouth to let him in. His tongue found hers, and she shuddered excitedly against him. His kiss was hot, hard and desperate, and she matched him with the same fierce desire. She freed her arms from where they had been pinned against his chest, brought them down and grabbed his buttocks, holding him against her. Kitty felt his hand slide down her thigh before he pulled her leg up to his hip. She wrapped it around him tightly as he ground against her, rubbing his erection against that oh so delightful spot between her legs, his mouth never moving from hers.

She gasped and jutted her pelvis forward, arching toward him, desperate for more. Between long, hot kisses, they were panting and clawing at each other's clothes, desperate for more of each other, each of them thrusting against the other with furious need.

She was close. Oh god, she was close. Just feeling Anthony's impressive erection grinding against her through multiple layers of fabric, she could feel herself swelling, and she was climbing higher and higher until...

"Fuck!" Anthony pulled back from her quickly, nearly sending her spiralling to the floor.

She grabbed the filing cabinet again to keep herself from collapsing in a heap.

"Fuck!" he said again, panting quickly.

"Well, I guess I did want to know," Kitty breathed, panting just as hard as he was.

He stepped back quickly.

"This is a fucking classroom," he snapped. "In a school. My school. God, what the fuck is wrong with me?"

"There's nothing wrong with you," Kitty panted as she desperately tried to catch her breath.

"No? He shot. "I've got ten missing kids and three missing teachers, at least one of whom has been violently attacked. Yet, instead of trying to find them, I'm almost screwing some gun wearing, spell-casting witch who's spent the past several years lying to me, in a fucking classroom of all places."

Kitty's heart slammed against her chest. She wasn't sure if she was angry, hurt or both. One look in his eyes, though, told her all she needed to know. He was furious.

"Anthony," she whispered.

"No," he snapped. "Don't Anthony me. Stop fucking around with me and do the damned job you came here to do. Find my people."

Kitty watched as he turned and marched to the door. He put his hand on the handle and then stopped himself.

"You know," She said mockingly. "Your grand gesture and dramatic exit would have been much more impressive if you weren't unable to leave here due to a massive hard-on."

She knew she was being cruel, but she couldn't stop herself. She was confused, angry and hurt.

"I realise that," he said, letting go of the door handle and turning away from her. "Can you leave, please?"

"In a minute," she answered, letting go of the filing cabinet and stepping toward him. "But first, I want my turn to say something. Since you and I were both active participants in what just happened, surely both of us get to have our say and not just you."

Anthony nodded but didn't turn around.

"Firstly, I never enjoyed having to lie to you," Kitty said. "In fact, I hated it. Lying to you, lying to my kids, it was awful. But those moments when we would talk about whatever issue needed addressing and I was relaxed, chatty, and a little flirty, that was real. That's who I am. The guns, the secrets, the missions, that's my job. It's not who I am; it's what I do.

"Kitty," Anthony started, but she cut him off. "This is my time," she reminded him. "Secondly, there are armed police and members of my team out physically searching for your people. They have been since just after I had my first vision, and that hasn't stopped. The rest of my team is researching, looking for CCTV footage, and manning the phones. They are coordinating all of the efforts to find out where the hostages are so that we can put together a rescue plan."

Anthony nodded and turned to face her, perching on the edge of a desk. He had his hands strategically placed to cover the still present but now slightly less prominent bulge in his trousers. "My job here is to work with you, issue instructions and check the progress of my team. But they really are the best in the country, and regardless of what I am doing, they are more than capable of doing this without me. I am here for you and the school, and as a mother, I am here for my own children too. I say what happens and when it happens, much like you."

"Like me?" Anthony looked puzzled.

"Do you run the reception desk, manage the school finances, teach every single subject, put together all of the timetables, and cook and serve the lunches?" She asked.

"I see your point," he said.

"I'm a General. It's like a headteacher, but I run a secret government organisation instead of running a school. So you need to know that nothing that happened in this room did anything to halt the progress of getting your people back. The only progress it halted was me going home to get the kids some clean clothes."

She smiled softly, and Anthony smiled back. She could tell he was having to force it, but it was a smile nonetheless.

"Finally," she said before Anthony could speak. "We did nothing wrong here."

Anthony frowned.

"I mean it," she told him. "You did nothing wrong. We are both stressed and emotional, and this needed to happen, so stop beating yourself up."

He opened his mouth to speak, but she held up a finger to stop him.

"I'll grant you, the location wasn't remotely suitable, but we are consenting adults, and we are in a semi-private location."

"Aside from the CCTV," Anthony cut in.

"Yes, aside from the… Fuck!"

"Say cheese," Anthony said as he pointed out the two security cameras in the classroom.

"I'll sort it," Kitty said, waving her hand dismissively. "The fact is, though, we're both in a highly stressful situation, and we're both carrying a lot of emotional baggage right now. There's no shame in admitting we're both upset, and we're both scared. There's no shame in seeking physical affection, comfort and pleasure to help process our emotions. But we can't do this again. At least not until this is over."

"You're right," Anthony said, standing up.

Kitty couldn't help noticing that his trousers were finally lying flat again.

"Oh, please say that again," she teased, quickly looking up at his face.

"I said it once, General," he mocked. "I'm not repeating it."

"Fair enough," she said as she walked toward the exit.

Kitty opened the door, and they left the room together, both of them avoiding eye contact with the armed police officers guarding the corridor.

Kitty stopped and turned to face Anthony as they walked along the oak-panelled corridor toward the meeting room where Kate was working.

"Ever been in a helicopter?" she asked with a grin.

Nine

As Anthony looked out of the window, he felt like a kid in a sweetshop. He'd never felt overly inclined to take a trip in a helicopter before. Now he was up there in the sky, looking down at his school and the surrounding streets; he wondered why he'd never wanted to do this before today. Sure it was painfully loud and a little cramped, but the experience was exhilarating, and the views were breath-taking. He had no idea how stunning the village he lived and worked in really was. Seeing it from the sky for the first time was an experience like no other.

Of course, there was a framed bird's eye print of the school in the main reception he had taken with a drone, but this was something else. As a keen amateur photographer, he'd been particularly proud of that photo. Now though, he felt as though he were the drone flying above the treetops, and Anthony wished he had his camera with him.

The hills, trees, fields, houses, and roads below looked so different from the sky. Up here, the village below looked new and inviting, and it felt as though he was seeing streets he'd run down countless times for the first time.

He'd always enjoyed trying new experiences, but they were usually physical challenges. Since riding in a helicopter wasn't a physical experience like climbing, kayaking or running a marathon, he'd never really thought it was something that would interest him. He realised now just how wrong he was.

As the sun began to set and dusk settled in the air, it could even have been romantic. That was if he and Kitty hadn't been sharing the ride with two members of her squad.

"This is amazing," he called over the headset to Kitty. "I wish I had my camera."

"It's a bit different being up here to sending your drone up for you, isn't it?" Kitty called back.

Kitty had warned him that the chopper would be pretty noisy even with the headsets, and they would have to be loud to hear each other. She hadn't been wrong. He felt like a young man in a crowded nightclub, trying to buy a drink over the noise of the music.

"Do you think we could come back up here sometime?" He asked. "I'd love to photograph all of this."

"Of course we can," Kitty answered. "But do you think you have enough wall space left at school for all of the prints you'll end up hanging?"

It was no secret that he was responsible for most of the photography that lined the walls at school. He'd even donated some pieces that had been auctioned at school events.

"I think I could find the room," he said as he turned his gaze from the window to Kitty and grinned at her.

"I did find a few inches of free wall space in the ladies loo earlier," Kitty called.

Anthony laughed. He knew she was being funny rather than unkind. It was well known that all of the facilities at school also had framed prints in them to add a more homely touch.

"Where are we going?" he asked, deciding it was time to change the subject and focus on the purpose of the trip.

"First," Kitty said, "We're going to give my neighbours a bit of a shock when I drop out of the sky and into the street where I live. Then, if you're comfortable with it, I thought you might find it useful to visit the abduction site. There may be something that you see that we've missed. After all, you know your staff better than anyone on my team does. You'll have a unique perspective on whether or not they were able to leave any sort of clue behind."

Anthony looked at her in surprise. Was she really after his opinion, or was she just trying to humour him? How could he really be helpful compared to her year of training? Surely that would be like him asking her how best to run his school. They were both excellent at what they did, but neither of them was qualified to switch roles.

"You want my opinion?" He asked.

She nodded. "In a case like this, it's important that no stone is left unturned. If you see anything, no matter how insignificant, you need to tell me." Anthony nodded and thought for a moment, pondering their discussion as the helicopter lowered significantly until everything below became much clearer.

"When you say drop out of the sky?" he asked.

"Watch," Kitty said, grinning. She clipped a carabiner with a black rope looped through it to the harness she'd put on before getting into the chopper. The helicopter started to hover slowly over the street below them, and she nodded to the soldier sitting opposite them.

Was she really going to jump out of an airborne helicopter?

"I'm ready, Corporal," she said as she gave the harness and rope one last tug to check everything was secure.

Anthony stared at Kitty for a moment. He was pretty sure he had a look of horror on his face, so he turned away to look back out of the window at the street below. People were standing on their doorsteps, watching the helicopter above them.

"You're actually going to jump out of a helicopter?" he asked.

"It's more like abseiling." She grinned at him.

"You've done this before, right?" he asked. He was still struggling with the fact that Kitty was this bad arse General and not this weak, vulnerable woman she'd presented herself as for so many years.

"Hundreds of times," Kitty assured him. "Remind me to tell you about Iraq when all of this is over."

"You were in Iraq?" Anthony asked, amazed.

"Two tours with the Army," Kitty shrugged.

"Secure and ready for drop off," a voice came through the headset, interrupting their conversation.

Anthony realised it was the pilot.

"Let's do this," Kitty said.

He watched as she rechecked her line as the Corporal in the back with them opened the sliding door from which she would descend. Kitty unclipped her seatbelt and stood up. She headed toward the open door and leaned out backwards. She looked down and then looked back at Anthony. He didn't dare look down. He wasn't afraid of heights, but he didn't want to witness it if something went wrong.

"Going down," she said, and with that, she lent right back and dropped from view.

"I can't believe she just did that," Anthony said to the Corporal, who was now feeding the line for Kitty. She's bloody insane."

"Yes, Sir, she is," the young soldier responded. "We don't call her The Fearless Witch for nothing."

"The Fearless Witch?" Anthony asked.

"Yes, Sir."

Anthony laughed, but he knew it wasn't true. Kitty wasn't fearless. He'd seen fear in her eyes. He'd held her while she trembled and cried in his arms. He'd never seen anyone as afraid as she'd been just a couple of hours earlier. Oh, she knew fear alright, and he never wanted to see her experience that kind of suffering again.

He had to give Kitty her due, though. She didn't let her fear hold her back. If anything, it motivated her and propelled her forward. Or, in this case, it propelled her down a rope from an airborne chopper. As Anthony thought about that, he wondered if anything could keep Kitty down for long. He'd been blessed enough to have plenty of strong women in his life, particularly his mother and his sisters, but he wasn't sure even they were as strong as Kitty was. Maybe instead of being called The Fearless Witch, she should be called The Strongest Witch.

An eruption of applause echoed through the street as Kitty landed gracefully on the road outside her house. There was no doubt about it; her cover was well and truly blown. In an instant, she'd gone from being a regular quiet mum to being the guy from the old Cadbury's Milk Tray adverts.

Kitty's next-door neighbour rushed to greet her as she unclipped the line from her harness. She tugged on it three times to let the young Corporal in the chopper above know that she was ready for him to retract it.

"Kitty?" Her neighbour had a questioning tone in her voice. "Are you some sort of super-spy?" Kitty took a couple of steps back, fully aware that she was armed and grinned at her friend.

"Something like that," she said.

"Does this have something to do with all of the police at S.H.P.?" her friend asked. "I was worried so about you and the girls. I've been calling and texting you."

"It has everything to do with the situation at S.H.P.," Kitty confirmed. "The girls and I are absolutely fine, though; thank you for checking. Sorry, I missed your calls, my personal phone is in my car. Unfortunately, I am unable to disclose any information at this time, but I'll tell you what I can just as soon as I can."

"I completely understand," her neighbour said. "You know me, I never press for information. I wait until it's offered, and I don't like gossip."

That was true. In all the time Betty had been Kitty's neighbour, she had never been one to seek personal information or gossip about other people's business. She had been a faithful and loyal friend over the years, unlike some of Kitty's neighbours who love nothing more than to gossip about everyone else. It was like Desperate Housewives in Surrey sometimes.

"People are going to ask you what we talked about here," Kitty said.

Betty nodded.

"Have some fun and make up something wild and outrageous," Kitty said. "Then, when I can, you and I will talk privately, and I'll fill you in on what I can."

Betty laughed. They both knew she wasn't the dramatic type and was no good at making up wild stories. Their children had grown up together, and it had always been Kitty's job to make up stories to tell the kids when they'd been camping out in the back garden.

"I'd hug you," Kitty said. "But I'm armed, and it would be a serious protocol breach."

"I understand," Betty said. "Be safe, Kit."

"You too, babe," Kitty said as she waved and sprinted to her house.

Once there, she opened the gate and walked along the garden path to her front door. She fished her keys from one of the pockets of her black cargo trousers and opened her red painted front door. She went inside, closed the door and leant against it for a moment. Her tumble dryer had finished drying the bed linen she'd put on before going out earlier, and the comforting smell of Bold and Zoflora drifted through the air. There really was no place like home.

Kitty knew it wouldn't take her long to grab what she needed. She always kept bags packed for herself and the girls. She needed a moment to herself, though, before she went back outside to the reality of the situation she was facing. She just needed a few minutes alone in the warmth and safety of her own home, so she walked across the hall and sat down on the second to last step of her cream carpeted staircase.

She dumped her keys down on the step next to her. She closed her eyes and rested her head against the bannister. For a while, she just sat there. She focused on her breathing as she tried to unpick the events of the last few hours in her mind.

Kitty thought about her interaction with Betty. She remembered herself stepping back from Betty. She remembered that she had told her that she couldn't get close because she was armed. Yet, she hadn't thought about that once when it came to Anthony. She'd been very up close and personal with him while she was armed. Dangerously close.

Why was she so willing to throw away her basic training for him? No, willing was the wrong word. It wasn't that she was willing; she just didn't think. Whenever he got close to her, she couldn't think. She could only feel, and that was a dangerous situation to be in. She didn't care about rules and regulations when he was around. She only cared about what was in her heart and the way her body reacted to his presence.

Ivy and Rose had joined Surrey Hills Prep when they were seven years old, seven years ago. That was seven years of being attracted to Anthony. Seven years of light banter and mild, harmless flirting. But it hadn't really been harmless at all. She'd dreamt of him more times than she could remember. She'd woken so many times in the night, her body dripping with sweat, her hands gripping the sheets, a fire between her legs.

The problem was, it wasn't just sexual attraction. Anthony was kind to her, even though she knew he hadn't thought her good enough for S.H.P. Even though she could feel his judging eyes on her when she wasn't looking. He was still always so kind and caring. Yet, he oozed strong masculine, alpha male energy. Those moments when she got to talk to him were few and far between, but she yearned for them. He would always ask her how she was and talk to her in such a way, he made her feel like she was the only woman in the world. Then, when they parted company, she would think about him for hours. She didn't just have a crush on him; she was smitten.

She hated that the relationship they had built up had been based upon a whole series of lies. Their relationship had, of course, been friendly but still professional. Yet, she'd often wondered if it could have been something more were she able to tell Anthony the truth.

There had been no directive to keep it a secret from him. Kitty could have told him the truth from the very start. It had been an option when she'd enrolled the girls, but she didn't want him to have to carry her secret or to put him in the position of lying to her daughters. God knew they had been subjected to enough lies over the years already. And so she had manufactured a series of lies to protect him, protect her kids and protect herself.

It hadn't really mattered to Kitty back then. She was sure her feelings had been very one-sided, and any possible interest he might have had was in her imagination. She assumed he was friendly like that with everyone, not just her. Until today, she was convinced there was no spark at all. Until today, she had burned for him privately without any genuine belief that he burned for her too. Today though, she had realised that she had been very wrong. Anthony wanted her as much as Kitty wanted him. When she'd been knocked on her arse by that last vision, she'd discovered how deeply he cared for her too.

Kitty stood and sighed. She couldn't think about this anymore. She couldn't think about him anymore. If she was going to get through this case, she would need to get her head in the game and put her heart and hormones in a box.

She headed to the coat cupboard under the stairs and pulled out three weekend bags and a suit bag. The girls could live out of their weekend bags for two weeks owing to her regimented packing skills. It was amazing how much she could pack into a small bag. Plus, with the laundry service for boarding students at school, they could last weeks if needed.

Her own bag contained all she needed for a week in the field, and her suit bag held a skirt suit, a trouser suit, two blouses and her formal uniform. All she needed was the pair of heels that she carried in her S.U.V. at all times, along with a spare pair of Army regulation boots.

She shut the cupboard door and headed into the living room where the girls had left their special teddies that morning. There was no way her kids would stay at school without those, so she quickly stuffed each bear inside the correct overnight bag and zipped them closed again. Finally, she picked everything up off of the cream leather sofa and headed back into the hall. She grabbed her keys off of the stairs and walked out the door, locking it behind her.

Once outside, she walked back into the middle of the road and tapped the homing beacon on her belt. Then she waited underneath the hovering chopper, aware that her neighbours were all still watching her. Some of them were holding out smartphones, and she knew she was either being photographed or videoed. That was a problem, but she'd have to worry about it once she was back up in the air. She'd make sure her tech team removed any traces of this incident from the web quickly.

The line dropped down, and she set the bags on the floor and clipped the line to her harness. Then grabbed the bags in her hands and managed to get enough of a grip to tug three times on the line to announce that she was ready to be hoisted back into the helicopter. Once again, her neighbours clapped and cheered as she lifted off and was pulled up into the sky.

As she reached the open door, Kitty threw each of the overnight bags and her suit bag into the chopper one at a time before being pulled back in herself.

"Well, I don't think my neighbours are going to look at me the same way again," she said as she unclipped the harness and sat back down in her seat. "It's time to move."

"Move?" Anthony asked as Kitty clipped her seatbelt back on.

"Yup," she said simply before announcing to the pilot that she was ready to get moving again.

"Move where?" he asked.

"As far away from here as possible," she shrugged. "Too bad, I love that little house."

"You can't just move, Kitty. What about the girls? Their friendships, their exams. What about…"

His voice trailed off, and Kitty sat there, willing him to finish that sentence. He said nothing, though, and she watched as he returned his attention to gazing out of the window.

"What about what, Anthony?" she demanded.

"Not now," he said, turning back and looking around the helicopter.

She had wanted to say, "Oh please. Do you really think these men don't hear bigger secrets and intelligence on a daily basis?" Yet, she didn't want to make him feel uncomfortable or embarrassed. He had always been such a strong alpha male. He was protective, authoritative, physically strong, respectable, well-educated, and a leader. Today she had swanned in with her new super leader identity and had practically castrated him there and then. She didn't want to keep adding to the humiliation.

Instead, she simply shrugged and said, "As you wish."

"E.T.A. ten minutes general," the pilot called over the radio and into the headsets they all wore.

"We're heading to the abduction site. Are you sure you're ready?" Kitty asked Anthony, changing the subject.

Anthony nodded, but he looked hesitant.

"You O.K?" she asked. "Any questions?"

"Just the one," he said. "Are we landing, or am I abseiling down?"

Ten

Kitty knew all too well that she should not be letting Anthony drop from the chopper, but she thought it would be good for him to try. Yes, he was a civilian, but he was also well accomplished and strong. He had trained in mixed martial arts, ran five kilometres every morning and trained in the gym every evening. He hiked, abseiled and had taken part in several triathlons and marathons. He hadn't told her any of this, of course, but she made a point of keeping tabs on the man who was responsible for her kids' safety. She had felt a little weird keeping tabs on him. It wasn't just him, though. She had run thorough background checks on everyone at S.H.P. Thankfully, it seemed the school was equally as careful when carrying out background checks on its employees. In the seven years her kids had been there, she'd never had any cause for concern.

Kitty was grateful for that, as she had never been able to figure out how she would go about telling Anthony if she'd found out anything untoward about his staff.

She knew it was a breach of procedure to let Anthony drop out of the sky, but she was willing to bend the rules just this once. He was undoubtedly competent enough after his years of climbing and abseiling experience. Besides, she felt she owed it to him. She wanted to give him back some control after how much she had taken from him in one day. Not to mention she wanted to see him wrinkle that damned pristine suit just once.

As Kitty sat there in her seat, she tried very hard not to check out Anthony's firm, muscled bottom as he climbed into the harness. He was swooping low due to the lack of headspace in the helicopter. His backside was leaning toward her, and it was just too delicious to resist. In fact, it wasn't just his butt; everything about him was too delicious to resist.

Anthony must have felt her eyes burning into him because he called through the headset, "Enjoying the show, General?"

Fuck!

"Just checking your straps aren't twisted," she lied.

"Straps, my arse," he chuckled.

"Your arse indeed," she smirked. She didn't have to see Anthony's face to know that he was turning a lovely, deep shade of pink.

"Get a room, you two," the pilot called over the radio.

"I heard they already did," the young Corporal helping Anthony into his harness called back.

"Oh, they did," the pilot confirmed. "It was a popcorn fest as we watched the live feed from the security cams."

Kitty could tell instantly that Anthony was furious. She saw his whole body tense and his knuckles turn white as he tightened his grip on the harness.

"Yep, that was pretty steamy stuff," the pilot continued. "Some of the guys there weren't sure whether to grab the popcorn or a box of tissues."

"Really, guys?" Anthony snapped hotly.

Uh-oh. He really was pissed off, and Kitty knew it was time to intervene.

"Ignore them," Kitty called through her headset. "They're just jealous. The only action these two get is from their own hands."

"You wound me, boss," the pilot said with a mock-hurt tone.

"I'll wound you in a minute, Rocket Man," Kitty said. "Give it a rest, yeah?"

"Alright, alright," the pilot said, laughing. "But seriously, Teach, you are one lucky dude. I've seen countless guys fall at the General's feet over the years, and she's stomped on all of them in her Army-issued boots. I'm telling you, not one guy has ever been lucky enough to even get a punch on the arm. I don't know how you managed to get close to her, but you really are one lucky guy."

Kitty wanted to be mad. Heck, she wanted to be furious, but she couldn't deny it was true. She'd had no interest in anyone other than Anthony for seven years. She'd not even looked at another man and had cringed every time one had looked at her.

"I don't know what to tell you boys," she called. "The heart wants what the heart wants. A guy has to be pretty damn amazing to get near me. I won't settle for anything less."

Anthony turned and looked at her, clearly shocked by her words. Had she said too much, or did he think it wasn't true? Kitty couldn't be sure.

"Is that true, General?" The Corporal asked. "You only like sexy headteachers?"

"No," she said, deciding to just be honest and get it over with so that they could change the subject. She knew Anthony would be mad as hell, but sometimes you had to throw a little something to the vultures to get them to stop circling.

"I only like one sexy headteacher," she clarified. "I've only had eyes for this man for seven years. No one else has even come close."

Secured into his harness, Anthony sat back down next to Kitty. She felt the heat radiating from him as he sat there glaring at her. Was he angry that she had shared her feelings?

"What about you, Teach?" the Corporal asked. "It's not exactly secret information that you've got a big hard-on for the general here."

"Or at least he did earlier," Rocket Man added. "A huge one."

"I think it's inappropriate to be discussing something highly personal and intimate between two people who clearly care about each other, with strangers," Anthony said. "The General and I obviously have much to discuss. Rather than talking about it so openly now, I'll wait and discuss it with her in private."

"And that boys," Kitty said, "Is why no one else even comes close."

She winked at Anthony, who was still frowning and looking thoroughly unimpressed.

Kitty reached over, squeezed his hand and shrugged.

"Sorry," she said softly.

"It's O.K," Anthony told her as he squeezed her hand back and smiled slightly. "We'll talk later."

"Two minutes to jump," Rocket Man called over the radio.

"Are you sure about this, General?" The Corporal asked. "It's not really procedure to let a civilian jump."

"I'm well aware, Corporal," Kitty called back. "But Teach has years of climbing and abseiling experience. He'll be fine."

"What?" Anthony asked.

She felt him pull his hand away from hers and watched his face as his smile quickly disappeared.

"You've been keeping tabs on what I do in my personal life?"

Nice one, Kitty thought. *Now he's mad at you again*. She needed to fix the situation before it was go time.

"Look at where you are, Anthony," she said as she casually waved a hand in the air. "Look at what I do for a living. Do you really think I don't keep tabs on every member of staff at Surrey Hills Prep? My job and my kids' lives depend on me knowing as much about your school and your staff as possible. I have to be sure my kids are safe, and I have to make sure they don't go to a school where any staff member could be a risk to this country."

"Fair enough," Anthony sighed. "But I don't like it."

"I'm pretty sure you're not supposed to like it," she told him. After all, who would like knowing they were being spied on by a government organisation?

"On a bright side," she added. "I've never had any concerns about any S.H.P. staff members. Everyone who has been through those doors for the past seven years has been clean. Your own background checks have been tip-top. I know you personally check into the backgrounds of every potential employee yourself. You've done a brilliant job of it."

"Oh," Anthony said. "I appreciate that, thanks."

His smile returned, and Kitty felt herself relax a little. She did not want to go into the field with someone who was angry at her or thought they couldn't trust her. What she'd said had been true, of course. However, she might not have thought to say anything before she'd accidentally told Anthony that she knew more about him than he realised.

The chopper lowered and slowed down.

"It's go time," Kitty said, and Anthony grinned.

Leaning over the side of an airborne helicopter and waiting to jump off wasn't exactly what Anthony had in mind when he got up that morning, but now that he was in the moment, he couldn't deny it was exhilarating. He looked over at Kitty, who was next to him, and his heart skipped a beat. How was it, the thought of jumping from a helicopter filled him with excitement, yet the idea of jumping into a relationship with Kitty scared the crap out of him?

Still, he couldn't deny it had made him feel good when she openly admitted to wanting him over any other man. That had made him feel respected, wanted, needed and powerful. No man could deny feeling good when a woman singled him out above all others. There was no more tremendous honour than hearing a woman say she wanted him and only him.

At the same time, that confession of her feelings made him uncomfortable and left him with an uneasy feeling in his gut. He had to remind himself that she was a parent with children in his school. It worried him how quickly he'd forgotten that in one afternoon. He was furious with himself for letting his guard down and throwing all of his professional boundaries out of the window at a time when he needed to be more professional than ever.

Yet something about this different side of Kitty had thrown Anthony completely off balance. She wasn't just a parent; she was an Army General and MI5 taskforce leader. She wasn't the vulnerable person he had assumed her to be but a warrior. She was so much more than he had ever known, and even before learning the truth, he had seriously craved her, despite his better judgement. He'd spent years forcing himself to disregard her and look down on her, even though it was against his very nature to treat any human like that. It had all been because he hadn't wanted to admit he was attracted to her, not because he'd thought poorly of her. He had been desperate to avoid facing the fact that he had feelings for her, so he had tried desperately to frown upon her. Yet, in those moments when they had met or talked on the phone, he'd been drawn to her. He'd even flirted a little.

Anthony had been at war with himself for years, and now he wasn't sure if knowing the truth made things easier or harder. He had no reason to force himself to look down on Kitty now, but he was also less able to resist her. And even though she was a high ranking official, she was still a parent and getting involved with her was a dismissible offence.

Yet, he had not only become involved, he'd done so in a classroom in full view of the school's CCTV cameras. And if Kitty's colleagues knew about it, he could be sure his staff knew as well. How long would it be before the Chair of Governors asked for his resignation?

"Are you alright?" Kitty was staring at him with a concerned look on her face. How lost in thought had he been?

"I was just thinking that this is probably the craziest thing I've ever done," he lied. Almost doing Kitty in a classroom was the craziest thing he'd ever done.

"Stick around, Ant," Kitty laughed. "I'll get you into all kinds of crazy trouble."

Oh, he knew that was true.

Wait a moment. Did Kitty just call me Ant?

No one dared to shorten his name. Anthony had hated it on the few occasions people had tried, and he had told them so. Yet, there was something oddly pleasant about the way it sounded when Kitty had said it.

He didn't have much time to think about it, though, as Kitty said, "Three, two, one, drop." He let go of the side of the helicopter and, just as Kitty had explained, began lowering himself down. He was hanging in mid-air, and it was incredible. He couldn't resist looking down at the street below him. *Holy shit*, this was spectacular. No wonder Kitty got such a buzz from it. Even the bitter wind whipping him in the face couldn't take away the magic of this moment.

Not magic, he scolded himself, science. This was physics, plain and simple. Oh, but the way Kitty had brought him to life hadn't felt like science. That had felt like the purest form of magic. That had felt like a rebirth. Finally, allowing him to be the person he was meant to be with the woman he was meant to be with. He couldn't explain the energy that surrounded them when they were alone; no science could.

When they were together, the air crackled, and anyone around them just faded into the background. When Kitty was near him, his heart raced, his body stirred, and he felt safe and terrified all at once.

He lowered himself to the ground where Kitty was already unclipped from her line and waiting for him. He unclipped his own line and stood there looking at the windswept brown curls that had escaped her helmet. Her hazel eyes were sparkling either from the wind or with excitement. He couldn't tell which.

Without thinking, he pulled her to him and kissed her fiercely. His hot and hard mouth teasing hers until her lips parted to allow his tongue to enter. She arched her body against his and snaked her arms around his neck, moaning softly in satisfaction. Oh man, she really was very good for him and very bad for him all at once.

Anthony knew if he didn't stop now, he would be hard again right there in the middle of the road, so he let go of her and pulled away.

"You enjoyed that then?" she asked after a few steadying breaths.

He looked at her damp, swollen lips and had to fight the urge to kiss her again. He stepped back in the hope that some distance between them would help him to control himself.

"I loved every second of it," he replied, not taking his eyes off of her lips.

"I meant the drop," Kitty laughed.

"Oh," he said. "That wasn't bad either."

Kitty swiped at his shoulder playfully, and he responded with a mock wince.

"What happened to us not being able to do that again?" She asked.

"You kissed me in my workplace," he told her. "It's only fair that I got to return the favour."

"Fair enough," she said. "Now, though, I need you to pay close attention."

He nodded. Kitty's voice had become suddenly serious, and Anthony knew that now was the time to drag his eyes from her puffy lips and get his head in the game. They had a mission, and if they were lucky, they might find something that would lead them to his missing staff and students.

"We're two roads from the abduction site," she told him as she began checking the tactical vest and helmet she had made him put on before they left the helicopter. "There are armed police and military personnel on-site, but I need you to stay close and listen carefully as between here and there, we're on our own. There may be snipers looming in the shadows, and it's my job to keep you alive."

"Got it," he said. He looked around instinctively, checking windows and rooftops.

"I'm sorry," she said as they started walking. "I know it's not very manly needing to be protected by a girl."

He noticed that Kitty was also looking around as they walked. He was surprised that they were walking so slowly and deliberately. He'd been expecting them to start sprinting.

"This is the twenty-first century Kitty," Anthony reminded her as they walked. "And I am quite comfortable with my masculinity, thank you. I'm not even slightly threatened by taking orders from a highly trained Army General. Your gender is irrelevant."

"Good," she said.

Her tone was weird, and she looked slightly taken aback when he allowed himself a brief moment to glance at her.

"Don't worry, I definitely noticed you're a woman," Anthony reassured Kitty. "It's just in this situation that matters less than your years of tactical training and experience."

"Oh, I know you noticed," Kitty said as she stopped just before a corner.

She held up a hand, and just as she had explained in the helicopter, Anthony knew to stop. Silently, he stood perfectly still as she stepped forward slowly and deliberately to peek around the corner ahead of them. Anthony glanced back at the way they had just come.

As he turned, something caught his gaze in the flat above the nearby carpet shop. Something in one of the windows caught the light of a streetlamp, almost dazzling him. He stepped back and refocused his vision, and looked back at the window above the carpet shop.

Everything felt like it was happening in slow motion. Anthony saw the dazzle again, only this time it was being raised by an arm. A wristwatch. A wristwatch and a hand holding a…

"GUN!" he yelled as he sprinted forward, running at Kitty, knocking her to the ground. He heard the sound of several loud pops as he fell on top of her and wrapped his body over her slender frame.

Pain seared through him as he clung to Kitty, holding her helmeted head down with his hand, his own head face down on the tarmac beneath them. Shots fired over and over as he grabbed Kitty's tactical vest. He rolled her around the corner and into the next road away from the view of the gunman. More pain. A burning, agonising sensation that swept through him in waves. Anthony rolled back onto Kitty, using his strength to hold her in place as she tried to wriggle free. He panted as the vile, bitter taste of adrenaline filled his mouth. The shooting stopped, and he knew they would have to get moving again before the gunman came after them in the street.

As he tried to pull himself up, pain tore through him, and his vision blurred. His heart was racing, and he felt sick and dizzy. He felt as though his soul and his body were out of alignment. In a brief, confused moment, he wondered if this was what Kitty would refer to as his chakras. He felt dazed, faint and disoriented.

As Anthony tried to force himself to focus, he looked down. He could see blood on his shirt. As his eyes started to roll and drift closed, the truth hit him almost as hard as the bullet had. He had been shot.

Eleven

Kitty pushed Anthony off of her and scrambled forward, commando crawling along the tarmac. She reached behind her, tucked her arm under the shoulder of Anthony's tactical vest and dragged him toward her. He was unconscious. At six foot four inches and well-toned and muscled, he was a lot of weight for her to drag by herself. Kitty was glad she had experience and adrenaline on her side as she managed to move him in four long pulls until she had him safely tucked behind a parked car.

Once out of sight of the buildings around her, she pulled a sidearm from its holster. She cocked it as she looked around repeatedly for any other shooters. There was nothing but cars, trees, houses and shops. In the distance, there was a petrol station and a park that was thankfully empty.

Then she reached into a small pocket in her tactical vest and pulled out a handful of black salt. She made a fist, gripping the salt tightly before bringing her hand down and resting her knuckles on the road in front of her.

Muttering to herself quietly, she said, "This is a time of desperate need, as the man before me continues to bleed. I raise this shield to keep us safe as we rest here in this dangerous place."

As Kitty finished chanting, she lifted her hand so it was palm up, uncurled her fingers and quickly threw her hand up in the air. As she pulled her hand away, the black salt sprinkled down around her and Anthony. As each rock of salt fell, red sparks formed around them, and she felt the energy of a mystical force field going up around them.

Kitty hadn't had time to ground herself, cast a protective circle or use a pre-prepared spell, yet she could feel the strength behind the magic she'd used. She knew the shield she'd conjured was powerful and would last until help arrived.

She looked down at Anthony, who hadn't regained consciousness and had still had blood oozing from his arm. Happy that her spell would hold, Kitty secured her gun and re-holstered it. Not even a rocket-propelled grenade would penetrate that force field. And if an R.P.G wasn't getting in, her bullets weren't getting out. There was no need for weapons anymore.

What she needed now was to assess Anthony and get him to a medic.

"Shit," Kitty exclaimed as she quickly examined Anthony's arm before checking his head was still being protected by his helmet. The Kevlar lined hard sat was still secured by the strap under his chin and showed no signs of being compromised. However, he was still bleeding.

After examining the helmet, Kitty was happy that Anthony's loss of consciousness was simply an episode of syncope caused by the extreme levels of adrenaline that came from being shot at.

The smell of blood nauseated her. Even after all these years since Uncle Tim's accident, blood was still a problem for her. It still filled her with a sense of dread, and the iron-rich smell of it, still made her feel light-headed and sick. Thankfully though, years of tactical training and experience had taught her to push those feelings aside. She knew how to bury those feelings and focus on the mission at hand. That was precisely what she did. She tapped the homing beacon on her belt, pulled the walkie talkie off of her vest, and spoke into the microphone while holding down the button that allowed her to be heard.

"This is General Kline. We have taken fire. I repeat, we have taken fire. I have a man down. I need a tac team and an emergency airlift evac at this location."

She discarded the radio and pulled out the first aid kit from her cargo pocket while gently taping Anthony's face.

"Wake up, Anthony," she demanded. "I need you to come back to me now."

He didn't respond.

"Dammit, Ant, wake up," she yelled.

Anthony stirred and groaned.

"Ouch," he mumbled. "My arm."

"You've been shot," Kitty told him as relief washed over her. Damn, it was good to hear his voice.

She ripped open the first aid kit. She wasn't worried about the blood loss that she could see; that was minimal. She was more concerned about him going into shock caused by the mental trauma he had just experienced. Being shot at could be a terrifying and life-changing experience.

Over the years, Kitty had normalised it. She'd been shot at more times than she cared to remember. Yet, it hadn't been like that the first time she'd been hit. The emotional trauma had taken considerably longer to recover from than the physical injury. Some people coped well; others were left with mental scars. She didn't know which way Anthony would go. No one did until it happened to them.

Kitty needed to keep Anthony talking, and she knew just how to do it. She grabbed the scissors from the first and kit and cut away the sleeve from his shirt.

"I like this shirt," Anthony groaned, wincing as she continued cutting the blood-stained cotton.

"You liked this shirt," Kitty corrected him as she set down the scissors and pulled a sterile pressure pad from the first aid kit. She tore open the packaging and pulled out the pad before pressing it hard against Anthony's upper arm.

"Fuck," he yelled.

His voice was strangled, and Kitty understood why. Having pressure applied to a gunshot wound was no fun at all. In fact, it was bloody agony. Still, this was no time for tea and sympathy. She grabbed Anthony's left arm and pulled it across his body, pressing it against the gunshot wound on his right arm.

"I need to you press here," she said, looking around her again for the sight of any more shooters.

"I think I'd rather bleed out," he grumbled.

Kitty wanted to scold him, but as she looked at his tired, dirty face, she could see a small smile playing on his lips.

"Inappropriate humour," she chuckled softly. "You can't be in that much pain then."

"It's hard to be in pain when I have such a beautiful woman nursing me," he whispered softly.

"You're delirious from all the blood loss," Kitty teased him. "Now hold this tightly. I need to check you for further injuries."

The next sixty seconds passed in a blur for Kitty. She felt around Anthony's body for further injuries while continuing to look around several more times for signs of either more shooters or her tac team.

There were three bullets lodged into the back of Anthony's tactical vest. One at his left kidney and two at his heart.

Sirens blared, a helicopter whirled overhead, voices grew louder, and Kitty breathed a sigh of relief. Within seconds soldiers and armed police ran toward Kitty and Anthony.

"Stop," she called as she held out her hands. "There's an energy shield surrounding us." Several more soldiers and police officers ran past them to the corner where they had been where they were shot at. Kitty chanted and clapped her hands twice above her head. She felt the barrier come down and nodded as people began to crowd her and Anthony.

In the distance, she saw nothing but heard everything. Shouting, orders to surrender, swearing and gunfire. Finally, she heard the reassuring words that the target was down and the area was secured. Now they could airlift Anthony out of there.

She turned her attention back to the first aid kit. She pulled out a sachet of saline and tore it open.

"O.K," she said to Anthony. "This is going to sting like a son on a bitch, but I need you to release the pressure on your arm so I can clean it."

Anthony nodded and moved his hand away. She pulled away the blood-soaked dressing and poured the saline over the gunshot wound. Anthony winced.

"That doesn't look too bad," she said. "The bullet didn't penetrate; it just grazed the surface. There's a team of medics that can stitch you up at the school, and you'll be as good as new in no time. You're going to be pretty sore for a while and will have some beautiful bruises where the bullets hit your vest, but you'll live to see another day."

"My first war wounds," Anthony mused. "Lucky me."

Kitty laughed as she opened a new sterile dressing and laid it over the wound site before opening a pressure bandage and beginning to wrap it around Anthony's arm.

"Ditch the suit jackets and wear short-sleeved shirts and you'll be able to show this off to everyone," she told him as a smile played on her lips.

"Great," Anthony sighed. "Then everyone can see that I managed to get myself shot."

"Actually," she corrected. "Then everyone will be able to see that your protective instincts kicked in, and you kept me from being shot."

She secured the bandage on his arm and gently squeezed his hand.

"You risked your life for me," she whispered. "I won't forget that in a hurry."

A round of praise from the surrounding officers and soldiers echoed around Kitty and Anthony.

"Great job, Teach, you're a hero."

"Nice one, Teach."

"Good work, Buddy."

"Thanks for keeping the General alive, Sir."

"Nice one, mate."

"Way to go, Teach."

"You did good."

"You should enlist, mate. You're a true hero."

"Alright, you lot," Kitty said as a litter and rescue bag were finally lowered from the chopper above. "Let's get Teach secure and back to school before he bleeds out."

Anthony glared at her.

"Kidding," she smirked. "But I don't want this lot making you big-headed."

"We heard you liked his big head General," one of the soldiers chirped.

"Oh god," Anthony groaned. "Not this again."

"Welcome to the Army, mate," another soldier teased.

"Pay no attention," Kitty told Anthony. "This lot are all guns and dirty minds."

It was only in those final moments on the ground that Kitty allowed herself to really stop and think about what had happened. Anthony had taken not one but four bullets for her. He'd risked his life to save hers. He could have been seriously injured or worse trying to save her. Even as she tried to work out how she would ever thank him for his unspeakable bravery, guilt and anger washed over her.

How the hell did she manage to miss the shooter in the first place? How could she have been so careless as to let this happen? It had been Kitty's job to protect Anthony, not the other way around. She had failed him, and he could have been killed as a result. What was she doing? How could she do her job when she was compromised by her feelings for the man she was supposed to protect? If Kitty was going to take down S.W.O., bring the hostages home and protect Anthony, she would have to stay as far away from him as possible. Then once all of this was over, she would move away, and she'd never see him again.

Anthony had declined morphine in the chopper and had made do with a couple of ibuprofen. He was in a significant amount of pain but wanted to maintain a clear head for the evening ahead. As long as members of his school were missing, there was no way Anthony was going to allow himself to get into a drug-induced fog.

He'd also point black refused to get into the rescue bag and litter. For the sake of what was essentially a few bruises and a graze, he would not go into a floating stretcher. Even after being reminded that he'd actually suffered significant blood loss and likely had bruising near his heart. Upon returning to school, Kitty had gone off for a debriefing. He'd been treated in the makeshift medical bay that had been set up in one of the classrooms.

Anthony had been back at school for over two hours, and exhaustion was starting to kick in. Still, he knew he couldn't sleep as long as he had missing teachers and students to worry about. Instead, he'd gone to the school gym. It had been converted into a shelter for the families of his missing students and staff. He spent some time with each family offering all the comfort and support he had to give, which hadn't felt like a lot under the circumstances. He'd passed around tea and biscuits because that was how Brits were expected to cope in such situations. Then he'd arranged for gym crash mats to be set out for young children to play and nap on.

After that, Anthony went to the main hall and spent some time with the on-site staff and students. He checked everyone, including the barrage of police and military personnel, had been fed. Then he'd arranged for his students to watch a movie with snacks on the main projector screen. This was usually reserved for Wednesdays and Fridays and not Mondays, but he thought it was warranted given the circumstances.

Anthony hadn't seen Kitty since they had gone their separate ways upon entering school and he was concerned. Instead, she had left him to his own devices, with Peter popping over to check on him a couple of times. There was no doubt about it; she was avoiding him.

He was a liability.

If Kitty hadn't have taken him into the field, she would have been more focused and better prepared, and she wouldn't have almost been shot. Taking Anthony into the field had been her idea, but he knew now she regretted it. He had let her down.

Things wouldn't have happened that way if he'd have just stayed at school where he belonged. Kitty wouldn't have been out there, and she wouldn't have almost been shot by some nut bag, gun-wielding terrorist.

Anthony needed some time to clear his head, he needed to eat, and he needed to stop feeling so damned sorry for himself. He decided to return to his living quarters and grab a shower and a sandwich. As he set his teacup down on the exam desk next to him, a sudden commotion startled him.

A loud scream.

Glass breaking.

Footsteps rushing.

Sobbing.

Students gasping.

Anthony stood from his seat at the back of the hall and looked for the noise source.

A trembling, crying teacher was being comforted by two colleagues. The water glass she had been drinking from was now in pieces on the floor. The tablet and headphones she'd been holding were now in the hands of an armed police officer.

Pain soured through Anthony as he broke into a run from one end of the hall to the other. He didn't need to see what she'd seen to know that the kidnappers had finally broken their silence.

"Sarah," he said to the distressed teacher as he came to a stop. "Are you alright?"

Sarah didn't answer. He pulled her to him and wrapped his arms around her.

Not letting go of the crying teacher, he turned to Matt and Gemma, his two deputy heads who had joined him at Sarah's side.

"Get every device away from every student night now," he told them. "No phones, no laptops, no tablets."

As he turned to look at the room full of frightened students, he could see some teachers had already begun collecting all of the girls' electrical devices.

"YouTube?" he asked, turning to the police officer holding the tablet as a soldier stepped forward with a broom to clean up the broken glass.

The police officer nodded.

Anthony pulled back from Sarah and gently sat her down in a chair. Gemma crouched down beside Sarah and put an arm around her.

"Go," Gemma insisted, glancing at Anthony. "We'll be alright here."

Anthony nodded and ran from the room, knowing he was leaving a well-handled situation in the main hall.

As he ran to his office, pain coursed through him. The bruising from getting hit by bullets, even with the protection of a tactical vest, was still incredibly painful. The medic had also told Anthony he suspected he had a couple of cracked ribs. They were either from the bullets or from the way he'd landed in a bid to protect Kitty from the gunfire. Either way, as he ran, the burning in his chest caused his lungs to sting sharply and, he struggled to regulate his breathing. He didn't feel like a man who ran five kilometres every morning. He felt like an overweight grizzly bear trying to get out of the way of oncoming traffic. Finally, he crashed into his office and threw himself down in the brown leather, swivel tub chair behind his desk. Ignoring the need to stop and rest for a few moments, He signed into his computer, picked up his headset and put it on. Every rise and full of his chest hurt, and he knew he needed to slow down and catch his breath. Yet taking the time to calm his breathing was time he didn't want to waste.

He pulled up YouTube on his computer and searched for anything that could be the video but found nothing.

"Fuck!" he hissed angrily. "Now, what do I do?"

As if by magic, his mobile phone pinged. Not the school phone used for communication with parents, but his personal one. He unlocked it and opened a text message.

YouTube responded very swiftly and removed the video. Check your email. My techs were able to grab a copy.

I really don't think this is something you should see, but I know you'll feel like you need to see it anyway. I won't stop you, but you need to know that this will be horrible for you to watch.

Kitty.

As he pulled up his email on his computer screen, he thought only very briefly about the fact Kitty had texted his personal number. Of course, she had his personal number. She probably knew what he had for breakfast. Still, as he opened the email and loaded the video, who had his phone number very quickly became the last thing on his mind.

Twelve

Anthony couldn't control the slight tremble in his hands as he loaded the video Kitty had sent him. Did he really need to see it, and if so, why? He knew he had nothing to gain from seeing people he cared about in distress, assuming the kidnappers even showed them in the video. Yet he couldn't help himself.

He needed to see for himself what condition they were in. He needed to see his colleagues who had become his friends over the years. He needed to see the young ladies he was charged with educating, nurturing and protecting.

It wasn't that he needed to see where he was failing in that capacity. It was more that Anthony needed to see what he needed to do to bring them back home safely. He needed to see what he had to do to care for them when they got back. As the video began to play, a knot formed in the pit of his stomach. He felt sick.

He couldn't stand it, yet somehow he couldn't cope with not seeing it either. He felt dizzy, and his entire body was shaking as the first scenes of the video began to play.

Thirteen young girls appeared before him, bound, gagged and crying. They were dirty, shaking and huddled together in a row. The hoods were gone. Anthony realised that was probably intentional. S.W.O. would want to display the faces of their hostages to prove they were alive. At either end of the row, Jenny and Clare sat in much the same condition, only Jenny was sporting a black eye, and a trail of blood trickled from her right temple. "Those bastards," he cursed angrily. "Those sick fucking bastards." Anthony had never in his life experienced the rage bubbling inside him now. It was a violent, sicking rage that spread through him like a cancer, consuming him and eating away at him. He wanted to grab each one of those terrorist scumbags by the throat and squeeze the life out of them.

Before he had the chance to calm himself, two armed and masked gunmen appeared on the screen, dragging Fitz between them. They threw him to the ground, and one of them yanked his head up, so it was in full view of the camera. "Fuck!" Anthony cursed again. Fitz was black and blue. *Fucking black and blue*. His nose was obviously broken, his lip was swollen and split, there was a gash on his head, and his sports kit was covered in blood and dirt. His eyes were both so swollen shut that Anthony couldn't even tell if he was conscious.

"Anthony Richmond," the guy who was obviously the lead gunman spoke with a strong cockney accent. "Listen up, Bruv. We've got your teachers, we've got your kids, and we've this dirty spade."

The racist gunman was referring to Fitz, of course.

"Literally though, unless you want your pussies to end up like thick lips here, Bruv, you'll get the feds to meet our demands. We know you are working with 'em. We have eyes on your school. For now, this lot is safe, but if we do not get our boys released from the prisons your shitty government has them at, we will begin battering these pretty teachers. We don't wanna do it, Bruv, as they're well fit, but we will and then we will shoot everyone here. Thirteen of our boys for twelve of your crop and your dutty pet dog."

"My fucking pet dog!" Anthony was horrified, furious and heartbroken all at once. Fitz was in the most awful, broken state and his students, Jenny and Clare, looked terrified.

The names of thirteen men scrolled across the screen. He'd heard of some of these men; their trials had been very public.

"You have until lunch tomorrow to give us what we want," the talking continued. "After that, we'll have some fun with the birds. That one," the gunman pointed at Jenny. "She's so thick she managed to fall down on her own. We didn't even touch her, Bruv, but we'll start with her first. She's too fucking thick to be a teacher anyway." Anthony winced as he focused on Jenny again. She was sobbing and shaking violently. Did this idiot who wouldn't even speak in proper sentences really just call her thick? *What a fucking joke.*

"And next time, Bruv," the video continued. "We ain't gonna miss when we shoot you. My brother is dead because of you. I swear down, I'm gonna kill you myself now, you dirty fucking cock sucking homo. If you want this lot to live, you will hand yourself over to my boys. I'll call you in the morning, Bruv and tell you where to go and don't even think of bringin' no pigs, you arse bandit."

He released Fitz, who fell to the floor and then stomped on his face. Then the video blacked out and ended.

"Son of a fucking bitch," Anthony roared as he stood. He grabbed the monitor of his computer, ripped out the wires and threw it across the room in an angry, violent rage. "I'm going to kill you, you filthy terrorist mother fucker. I'm going to squeeze the fucking life right out of you."

He threw himself back into his chair, pain coursing through his body, put his head into his hands and cried. He hadn't cried since he was a child, but now he couldn't stop the hot, angry tears that poured out from deep within his very soul. He cried so hard he found it hard to breathe and kept making himself retch.

Anthony cried for his students, he cried for Jenny and Clare, he cried for Fitz, he cried for the families who were in the school sports hall waiting to get their loved ones back. He cried because he was in pain, and he cried because he was just exhausted.

Eventually, the gut-wrenching tears settled into quiet sobs.

He wasn't sure how long he sat there, but at some point, the tears dried out completely, and his breathing steadied as he grew calmer. He opened his eyes, got to his feet and looked around the room. He winced as he noticed the smashed P.C. monitor in pieces at the other end of the room.

Somehow his excellent throwing skills had allowed the monitor to hit the far wall and ricochet back off of it before crashing to the floor. The fact that it had been a remarkable shot, given how much pain he was in, did nothing to soothe him. On any other day, he would have been impressed by his throwing skills. Then again, on any other day, he would never have become so angry that he felt the need to damage school property in the first place. He'd never been one for temper fits or violent outbursts. He hated violence, yet he had stood there screaming into his empty office that he wanted to squeeze the life out of another human being. What was happening to him?

"Kitty," he said to himself firmly. "I need to see Kitty now."

He crossed the room and reached for the door handle. He took one last look at the computer monitor he had utterly destroyed and the damaged wall before he opened his office door. Kitty was leaning against the wall directly across from his open door. He looked at her and frowned.

"How long have you been there?" Anthony asked impatiently.

"I was standing here when I texted you," she said.

"And how long ago was that?" he demanded.

"About an hour and a half ago," she admitted.

"You've been standing here for that long? Didn't you think to come and talk to me about all this mess?" Anthony could feel his frustration rising, and he had to remind himself to take some calming breaths. Kitty wasn't the enemy here. She was the one who was tasked with taking down the enemy. She was the one he was counting on to bring his people home alive.

Kitty gently pushed herself off of the wall and motioned her hand at Anthony's office. He stepped aside to allow her access and then closed the door behind them both.

"You needed time to process your anger and your grief in private," she said, shrugging. "I knew that once you were ready to talk, you'd open the door and come looking for me. I wanted to be right there when you did."

Anthony stopped frowning and allowed his features to soften. He actually really appreciated that she had given him the time and space to have his meltdown privately. He wasn't one for public displays of emotion. He would not have welcomed the audience at a time where he had been particularly vulnerable. That being said, he wasn't sure it was really all that private when she had been standing right outside the door.

"Thank you," he said as he waved a hand toward the sofa by way of an invitation for Kitty to sit.

He watched as she made an effort to look up when she walked over to the sofa, as though she hadn't noticed the smashed computer monitor on the hardwood floor. She also made no mention of it as she sat down on the sofa, and he perched himself on the edge of his large mahogany desk. He was grateful Kitty had chosen to ignore the obvious elephant in the room. It spared him the embarrassment of having to admit that he had launched his computer monitor mid-tantrum.

"What do we do now?" Anthony asked as he picked up a pen from his desk and began to roll it between the palms of his hands.

"We keep doing what we have been doing," Kitty told him. "We keep searching every warehouse with any connection to fish within an hour and a half of here."

"No offence, Kitty, but that isn't enough," Anthony told her as he placed the pen back on his desk.

"It'll have to be enough," Kitty said. "We will not negotiate with terrorists."

"Not even to save ten innocent children?" He asked hotly. Once again, he could feel his temper rising, and it worried him how little control he had over his emotions. He had never been so highly strung.

"If we release prisoners who have been rightfully convicted, Anthony, we run the risk of becoming vulnerable to several terrorist organisations. Not only that but if we release this lot, what's to stop them from asking for another thirteen and then another thirteen. We currently have over a hundred S.W.O. terrorists locked up in the U.K. If we give in now, when will it end?"

He knew her reasoning made sense, but it didn't make it any less of a bitter pill to swallow.

"What if we give them me?" he asked.

"No way in hell," Kitty shot back.

"But they want me," he protested. "You could use me as bait. Use the blood to blood spell that Kate told me about."

"And if they decide to just shoot you on the spot rather than taking you to the warehouse," Kitty said firmly. "Then what happens? No, I'm sorry, Anthony, it's not happening."

"There must be something we can bloody do," Anthony snapped.

"We're doing it, darling," Kitty said softly. "I promise you, we are doing everything possible to find your people. As soon as we do, my team and I will go in and your people out."

"I just wish there was more I could do," Anthony sighed.

"You are doing what you need to do," Kitty assured him. "You are here, working with us and supporting everyone here who needs you."

"It isn't enough," Anthony said again.

"You look beat," Kitty said softly. "You're tired, in pain, and emotional. You need to start taking care of yourself. What time did you last eat or drink anything?"

"Lunchtime, I guess," he shrugged. "Although I had half a cup of tea before the video."

"You need to eat and drink something," Kitty said, getting back to her feet.

"No," he said firmly. "I'm fine. Thank you."

"Anthony," she started, but he cut her off.

"Are they eating?" he asked.

"Who?" Kitty asked in response.

"My staff and my kids. Do you think they've been fed?"

"Not likely," Kitty admitted softly.

"Then until we get them back, I'll go without too."

"Anthony, please reconsider."

"No," Anthony said impatiently. "That's the way it is, Kitty. Now you can either get off my case or get out."

Kitty looked taken aback, and Anthony instantly regretted being so rude.

"You've been shot," Kitty reminded him. "You've been through physical and emotional trauma. You need to look after yourself properly if you're going to continue caring for the staff, students and families who are still here. They're relying on you to be strong right now."

"I don't feel very strong right now," Anthony admitted.

"I know, darling," Kitty said softly. "You've been to hell and back today."

"I think I'm still there," he whispered.

"Then trust me to help you to find the way out," she said as she finally shuffled back on the sofa, twisted and popped her legs up on the leather. Anthony didn't say anything about Kitty making herself at home. He was sure she felt as drained as he did, and she was probably a little bruised after he had thrown her to the ground and pinned her.

"They didn't try to kill you today," he said quickly.

"Huh?" Kitty asked.

"They didn't want you," he told her. "They wanted me. They hadn't fired at anyone else who had walked past that spot all afternoon. They were waiting for me. They wanted to kill me because they have it in their heads that I'm gay."

"I know," Kitty sighed as she crossed her feet at her ankles. "I'm so sorry."

"You're sorry?" he asked, puzzled. "Why are you sorry? I could have got you killed today Kitty. I almost did."

"That's not true," Kitty said firmly. "I was in no real danger. I had my vest and helmet to protect all the major organs. I would have been fine."

"Please don't patronise me, Kitty," Anthony said. "We both know that one bullet to the femoral artery, and you would have bled out before help got to us."

"Don't you believe it," she said. "Speaking from experience, you can survive at least a few minutes if you keep the pressure on until help arrives."

"Experience?" he asked.

"That stab wound I mentioned earlier," Kitty said, swinging her legs off the sofa and rising to her feet. She ran her hand up her thigh, and for the first time since she'd entered the room, it actually registered with Anthony that she had changed her clothes.

Gone were the cargo pants and tactical vest. Now Kitty was wearing a black pencil skirt with a dignified side split, a white button-up blouse with a loose open collar and black pumps. And for the first time all day, she wasn't wearing a gun. Her curls were no longer trying to escape her ponytail and were instead smooth, shiny and cascading around her face.

Of course, she still had her two signature skinny plaits. They were tied with the usual hair elastics, with crystals attached to them. She wouldn't be Kitty without those. But he'd never seen her dressed so formally before, and she looked stunning.

"You've changed," he murmured as she hitched up her skirt and gently tugged her stocking free of the suspender belt holding it in place.

"You noticed, huh?" she responded as she freed her stocking and rolled it down, exposing a now naked thigh.

"Kitty," he said as he felt panic and something else rising. "What the hell are you doing?"
"Showing you my scar," Kitty shrugged, seemingly oblivious to his sudden discomfort. "Here," she said, walking over to him and taking his hand in hers. "Feel it."
"I'm good," he said as he firmly pulled his hand back.
"Don't be such a baby," she laughed. "It's just a scar; it won't bite you."
With that, she took his hand once more, pulled it to her thigh and held his fingers in place over her scar.

Thirteen

As soon as Anthony's hand touched her bare skin, Kitty knew she'd made a terrible mistake. She felt his body as well as her own tense up at the exact same time. She felt the air in the room crackle, and she felt goose bumps pop up all over her. Her face grew hot, as did the most intimate area between her legs. Had she been foolish enough to think Anthony could touch her without her body reacting like this? Deep down, had she wanted him to touch her because she knew how amazing one slight touch from him would feel?

Kitty wasn't sure. She wasn't sure of anything. She was conflicted and confused. Did she want Anthony to keep touching her, or did she want him to stop?

"Kitty," Anthony warned. "Stop."

She pulled away from him and stepped back quickly. Too quickly. Then everything suddenly felt as though it were happening in slow motion. Her foot caught on the leg of Anthony's large desk, and she stumbled. She felt herself falling backwards and knew she would land with an ungraceful thud on his office floor.

Somehow though, she didn't end up on the floor in a heap. Instead, she found herself wrapped in Anthony's arms as he held her tightly. He had grabbed hold of her to stop her from falling. She'd known it had been an act designed purely to protect her, but as he pulled her against him, he growled, and she felt her body respond as fire shot through her.

For the briefest moment, Kitty allowed herself to rest her head on his hard, muscled chest and drink in his scent. She could feel herself drowning in him and forced herself to pull away from his grip.

"We keep coming back to this," she said, this time stepping away from him more carefully and deliberately. "But I can't get involved with you, Anthony. Not now, not after everything."

"Everything?" he asked.

She nodded. "It's too much. You, my feelings, Jack. I just can't do it again."

What was wrong with her? She'd craved this man for so long, but now that the opportunity to be close to him was finally here, she found she didn't want to take the risk. She didn't want to go through the heartache all over again.

She stepped around to the other side of the large mahogany desk, desperate to put some space between her and Anthony.

"Jack?" he asked, his expression softening.

Kitty knew saying his name aloud would lead to questions, but she needed to do it anyway. She needed Anthony to understand why she couldn't get involved again.

"Rosie and Ivy's father," she sighed.

"I know," he said quietly. "You've just never mentioned him before."

"I couldn't," she admitted. "I couldn't face talking about Jack, not to you."

"And now?" Anthony asked.

"Now, you need to see why this can never happen," Kitty said firmly.

She came back around the desk and stood next to him. She was sure Jack would be enough of a barrier between them to keep them apart, but as she leaned back on his desk, she made sure to leave enough of a gap between them that their bodies didn't touch. She stared ahead at the broken P.C. monitor at the other end of the room just to avoid turning to look at Anthony.

Kitty didn't want to make eye contact with him. She didn't want to see his sympathy. She wanted nothing to pass between them at that moment, other than an understanding of why they couldn't be together.

"Tell me," Anthony said softly. "Tell me about Jack."

"Jack Kline was the love of my life," Kitty whispered. "We met on the first day of basic training, and we were inseparable from the very beginning.

"At first, it was just friendship. We didn't know anyone, so we agreed to make a pact. We'd be best friends and take care of each other. We spent every spare minute together, and then one day after six months, he texted me. We were sat right opposite each other in the pub, but he pulled out his phone and texted me to tell me he loved me. I texted him back to tell him that I loved him too. He stood up and walked over to me. He pulled me to my feet and kissed me hard."

She stopped to take a breath and try to gauge Anthony's reaction. She wasn't sure how he would react to all she had said so far and all she still had to say. She needed him to hear the truth, but she didn't want to hurt him.

"It's O'K," he said as if sensing her unease. "Go on."

She nodded and continued.

"We kept our relationship private for a year, or at least we thought we had. Then, a month before we were due to ship out to Iraq, our C.O. came to us. He told us we should marry before shipping out so that if anything happened to us out there, we'd have no regrets. So he went to his C.O. and got permission for us to marry, and we obtained a special licence and married a week later."

"Peter was the C.O., right?" Anthony asked.

"Peter Lee, the Chief Superintendent."

"How did you know?" Kitty asked, allowing herself a brief moment to glance up at Anthony.

"I've seen you two together," he said. "You didn't become as close as you are without going through some serious shit together."

"We're not…." Kitty started. "We've never…."

"I know that," Anthony laughed softly. "I've seen you together. You're as close to him as I am with my sisters. He's your family."

Kitty looked up at Anthony and smiled. He understood the dynamic between her and Peter perfectly. She should have known he would. She'd seen enough banter between him and Fitz over the years to realise they had a similar relationship.

"Tell me more," he said softly. "Keep going."

"We served two tours in Iraq and one in Afghanistan together. Peter, Jack and I. As you said, he was like a big brother to us and not just our C.O. Then the time came when Jack and I wanted to start a family. We used the inheritance from my parents to buy a house, and my discharge was approved. It didn't take long for me to fall pregnant, but by the time I realised Jack was already back in Iraq. He'd joked and called it his farewell tour before his own discharge came through. I was going to surprise him with the pregnancy when he came home six months later. I was going to meet him when he arrived back at base with a round baby bump, and then he and Peter were both going to join the police force."

"What happened?" Anthony asked.

"I went for my twelve-week scan and discovered I was having twins. I got home from my appointment, and Peter was waiting at the door. He had been promoted and hadn't gone to Iraq with Jack. While it wasn't uncommon for him to stop by, he wasn't wearing his civvies this time. He was in his dress uniform, and an Army Chaplin was with him."

Anthony sighed softly, and Kitty knew that this would be the moment if she looked at him now. This was when she would see the sympathy she was desperate to avoid. She'd seen it from so many people over the years, and in some way, it gave her comfort. Yet, she couldn't stand to see it coming from Anthony. She didn't need sympathy from her almost lover over her dead husband.

"Roadside bomb," Kitty said simply as she pulled her shoulders back and lifted her head a little higher in a bid to look stronger than she felt.

Anthony went to reach for her hand with his own, and she pulled back.

"Don't," she shot. "I don't want sympathy. Not from you. I couldn't stand it."

Anthony nodded silently and moved his hand away.

Kitty looked up at him. He looked hurt. She hadn't wanted to hurt him, but she just couldn't take comfort from him. She couldn't accept his sympathy. She couldn't find comfort over the loss of Jack in another man's arms.

"He didn't need to do that last tour, you know," Kitty told Anthony as she turned her gaze to a spot on the hardwood floor, where two little notches sat in the woodgrain. They looked like they were chasing each other but never quite catching each other.

"I told him to go off and have one more tour so that when he left the Army, he'd have no regrets. He died not knowing he was going to be a father because I'd kept it from him. I shouldn't have let him go. We were trying for a family. I should have just said no. Told him to get his discharge papers and get out when I did. My biggest regrets are not pushing him to discharge with me and not telling him he was going to be a father. I loved him, and I lost him, but my girls lost him before they even got to love him."

"You can't blame yourself for that, Kitty," Anthony told her.

"I don't blame me," she said hotly. "I blame the terrorist scum who blew up my husband. There's a big difference between regretting your choices and blaming yourself. I have to live with the choices I made. They led to my husband dying alone in a war zone without knowing he was going to be a father. I made those choices, but I am not responsible for the son of a bitch who killed him."

She wasn't sure she was making any sense, but she just let the words flood out of her anyway. She had to say what was on her mind and what was in her heart.

"I can't be involved with you, Anthony," she said, finally getting to what she actually needed to make clear to him. "I took you into the field today, and it could have killed you. My life, my job, it's too dangerous to bring you into it. I can't live a life of more regrets. I'd rather have one regret when it comes to you, and you be alive than have many, and you be dead."

"Don't I get to decide what's right for me?" Anthony asked, sounding a little annoyed. "What gives you the right to decide what's best for me?"

"Don't you get it?" she snapped. "You could have died out there today."

"I was shot at several times, Kitty," he reminded her sarcastically. "I'm pretty sure I get it. And if that wasn't enough, the most recent death threat might have been a hint."

"Damn it, Anthony," she yelled. "I won't love you and lose you. I've done it once, and I won't do it again."

Kitty stared long and hard at the broken computer monitor, trying to piece it back together in her mind's eye. There were little pieces all over the floor, and she knew it was a hopeless case just as she knew she and Anthony were a hopeless case. Any chance of a relationship they might've had was as broken as the screen on the floor.

"I'm not asking you to love me, Kitty," Anthony sighed, his voice growing softer. "I'm not asking you to commit your life to me. I'm asking you to trust me to make my own choices. I'm asking you to just be present with me in the moment. We may decide after all of this is over that we really don't like each other after all."

"God knows we argue enough for that to be true," Kitty said bitterly.

"But Kitty, we will never know unless we try in the here and now to find comfort, support, friendship and faith in each other."

Kitty didn't want to try. She wanted to run away and never look back.

"I can't," she whispered. She could feel the hot sting of tears welling in her eyes. She had dreamed of them having a conversation like this. One where they shared their feelings and then finally made love to each other.

"I could have died today," Anthony said quietly. "At that moment, my biggest regret was pulling away from you earlier. Not finishing what we'd started. Not making love to you when I had the chance."

"Don't," she told him firmly. The word was strangled as she tried to hold back the tears threatening to spill over.

"Neither of us knows what's coming next, Kitty," he said. "Not even you with your powers of premonition. Either one of us could get hit by a bus tomorrow."

"Nice," Kitty said sarcastically.

"My point is, we don't know when our time is up," Anthony said. "And not all deaths are caused by terrorists.

"No, they aren't," Kitty agreed.

She knew her resolve was fading; she could feel it. The urge to run away was being replaced by the desire to pull Anthony to her. Confusion swept over her, and she didn't know what the right choice was anymore. She wanted Anthony, but she didn't want to give her heart to him just for it to end up broken again.

Kitty stood up and tried to move away, but she found her wrist being gripped gently but securely by Anthony's hand. As he tugged on her wrist gently, she turned to face him. And as he lifted his other hand and gently wiped the tears from her face, she felt herself stepping closer to him. Was he right? Hadn't she had the same thoughts when he had been bleeding in the road? Hadn't she also been filled with regret? Hadn't she also wished they had finished what they'd started in the bloody maths classroom earlier?

This moment between them had been her dream. In a few days, she would be leaving, and she wouldn't be coming back. And at that moment, she knew. She knew she couldn't go without being with Anthony, just once.

"I need you, Kitty," he breathed.

"I need you too," she choked.

It was finally time. Kitty wasn't going to wait another moment to be in his arms.

Fourteen

Anthony just stood there for what felt like an eternity, staring into Kitty's eyes. He'd dreamt of making love to Kitty so many times over the years. He'd hated himself for it. He'd hated that he had even thought about her in that way. He was a headteacher, and she was a parent. He was pretty sure he'd be sacked on the spot for just thinking it if the Chair of Governors had been able to read minds. There was never a situation where it was acceptable for the head to screw a parent, but he no longer cared. He and Kitty had wasted too much time, and after the events of the last several hours, he was no longer prepared to sacrifice his happiness for his job.

Now, as she stood there, Kitty's wrist tucked neatly into his hand, their eyes locked together, her pulse racing beneath his fingers; Anthony knew. He hadn't only been fantasising about Kitty; he'd been falling in love with her.

Oh, he'd tried to fight it. He'd wanted to dislike her, tried to reject everything about her, but she had become engrained in his heart. Anthony realised now as he stood there, gently holding onto Kitty's wrist, that he had been in love with her for a very long time. Gently, he pulled her to him, and she came willingly.

"I'm leaving," she whispered, her breath catching in her throat. "When all this is over, Anthony, I'm leaving this place, and I'm not coming back."

Her words hit him like a sledgehammer.

He didn't want her to ever leave. He wanted to stand by her side for as long as he was breathing. He also knew that she needed to be unknown as long as she did the job she did. By now, every member of staff in his school knew the truth about her. Everyone on the road where she lived would know about her by now as well.

She had to protect her family. He knew that. He could face heartbreak to keep Kitty safe. What he couldn't do was let her go without ever having held her close to him as he filled her and moved inside her. He couldn't let her go without being with her just once, even if it ripped his heart to shreds.

"Be with me now, Kitty," he breathed. "If you're leaving, I don't want us to have any regrets. If you walk out that door now, I won't try and stop you, but I'll always regret not making love to you."

The words he spoke came from his heart. He had wasted enough time by lying to himself for seven years. He'd kept Kitty at arm's length for too long. Now he needed this moment with her because when she was gone, he'd have only memories.

"I can't," Kitty sighed. "I can't do that to you."

"I want you," he growled. "I don't want you to leave without me showing you how much I want you and for how long I've wanted you."

"I want you too," she whispered. "I always have."

"No regrets," he promised. "Just our own goodbye."

She nodded slowly, and he pulled her closer still and cupped her face with the hand that wasn't still holding her wrist. Her beautiful soft skin was still damp from tears, and he wanted to kiss every last trace of them away. He wanted to kiss all of her hurt away and fill her with nothing but his love for her.

"You're so beautiful, Kitty," he told her softly, as he moved his hand to the back of her head and gently brought it forward before his mouth claimed hers.

Anthony's kisses were slow and gentle. He wanted Kitty so much it caused him to physically ache, but he had to savour this moment. He had to do it slowly and do it right because when this was over, he'd have nothing but memories and a broken heart. He held her against him as he claimed her mouth, still keeping hold of her wrist.

He moved his mouth from hers. He gently kissed his way along her jaw, to her earlobe and down her throat. He let go of her wrist and scooped his arm around her, his hand pressed firmly on her back, his other still cradling the back of her head. He drew his lips up her face, gently kissing away the last traces of her tears. Then he found her mouth again and kissed her harder, deeper. Anthony pressed Kitty against him as his tongue met hers, deepening the kiss. He felt her grind against his erection as his tongue continued to dance with hers. He broke free of her mouth and laced her throat with more hot, wet kisses.

"Anthony," she breathed, arching her head back and her hips forward.

"Kitty," he growled deeply as his mouth came away from her throat, and he slid both hands to her waist. Carefully, he manoeuvred them both so that he was longer pressed against the desk; she was. He slid his hands down her thighs slowly. When he dragged them back upward, he brought her skirt up with them, pulling it up to her hips, exposing her stockings, suspenders and thong. He cupped her bare bottom with his hands, squeezing gently as he kissed her. His mouth claimed hers greedily. He was hungry for her, desperate for her.

Without moving his mouth from hers, Anthony slid his hands up to Kitty's waist. He lifted her and sat her on the desk and pulled her legs apart. He pulled back and gently unhooked her stockings from the suspender belt she was wearing. He was slow, taking his time, savouring the time he had with her.

Kitty groaned impatiently.

"Not yet, baby," Anthony whispered. "I have so much I want to do to you. There's so much pleasure I want to give you."

He moved closer and slid her toward him so that she sat just at the edge of the desk. Kissing her once more, he pulled on her blouse until it was free of the waistband of her shirt. One by one, he slowly undid each of the buttons, kissing her the whole time, letting his tongue find hers. Finally, he pealed the garment from her body and let it fall onto the desk behind her.

He slid his hands between their bodies, reaching for her breasts over her lace bra. Gently, he began to stimulate her nipples over the lace, tugging them and teasing them, gently at first and then firmer until she moaned in pleasure.

Finally, when he was sure he would break if he didn't feel her naked breasts in his hands and mouth, Anthony reached behind her and unhooked her bra. He pulled it away, allowing Kitty's breasts to fall free. He stepped back and gazed at her for a moment, taking in her beauty as his erection begged to be as free as her naked breasts.

Oh god, he wanted her. He was bulging out of his trousers in a hot frenzied need for her. Still, though, he took his time, savouring every moment he had with her. He was drowning in his desire for her and didn't want to hold back any longer, but he knew if he didn't, it would be over, and she would be gone from his life. He had to make this last as long as possible. He had to have her with him for as long as possible. He resisted the urge to tear open his trousers and reminded himself to focus on her. He allowed himself a brief moment of temptation as he pressed against her and ground his erection against the warm spot between her legs. It was almost his undoing, but as Kitty wriggled and squirmed against him, he knew she wanted more.

"I'm yours, Anthony Richmond," Kitty said breathlessly, leaning back onto her forearms. "Come and get me."

And he did. His mouth claimed Kitty's left breast with a greedy hunger as Anthony's left hand cupped and caressed the right breast. He tugged, squeezed and kneaded her nipple gently between his thumb and forefinger.

Anthony felt Kitty arch against him and wrap her legs around his waist, pulling him closer to her. Once again, she was pulling his erection to that place between her legs. He ground against her, and she responded by bucking against him. He pulled back slightly and slid his hand down between her legs. Her thong was already damp, and she was warm.

Gently tugging her underwear to one side, Anthony slipped a finger inside Kitty. She was hot, wet and ready. He slipped in a second finger and, on the outside, began to massage the already swollen spot between her legs. Harder. Faster.

"Oh my fuck," Kitty cried out as she squirmed and bucked against him.

She was restless and needy, and Anthony knew she was close. She wanted him, she needed him, and it made him feel intoxicated. He rubbed her harder and faster still, and she cried out again.

"Oh god, Anthony," Kitty cried. "You're going to make me come."

"Yes," Anthony breathed, unsure of how much longer he could maintain control. "Come for me, baby, let me feel you."

She cried out his name as she exploded around him. He could feel the violent spasms as she clenched around his fingers. He pressed in further, rubbed harder, and she cried out over and over again, coming around his fingers.

Kitty clawed at Anthony's shoulders through his shirt and arched her back, bucking against him, panting, groaning and crying out until slowly she began to slow down and settle. For a brief moment, she just lay there on his desk, spent.

Oh god, he needed her. He had to feel her do that again, only this time with his shaft inside of her. Yet, Anthony knew he needed to wait just a little longer.

He looked around the room for anything that would distract him. He needed something to stop him from ripping open his trousers and ploughing into Kitty with everything he had until he too was spent and empty. He noticed that Kitty's blouse was now in a crumpled heap on the floor. The stack of paperwork that had been neatly piled on his desk was now scattered on his chair, the desk and the floor. But what he really noticed were Kitty's naked breasts, round and full and deliciously tempting.

Anthony wanted them again. He wanted to feel them in his mouth and tease them with his hands. He wanted to make her cry out his name again and feel her come undone once more.

He ran his hands along her shoulders. He slid them down her body until her breasts were cupped in his hands. This time he brought his mouth down to her right breast. He licked it and nibbled it as his left hand teased her right breast, tweaking her nipple and tugging it gently.

Kitty groaned in pleasure as he continued to tease her breasts, and he pulled his mouth away from her. He stood straighter and pressed against her. Once again, Anthony ground his erection into the most intimate spot between her legs. He continued to massage both her breasts with his hands. She pulled her legs up and wrapped them around him, pulling him closer.

"Oh god, Kitty," he panted.

"Make me come, Anthony," she pleaded. "I need you to make me come again."

He tweaked her nipples harder and continued to grind against her as she gripped the edge of his desk and bucked against him.

"Fuck Anthony," she cried out. "You're so hard."

He slid his hands down her body and settled them on her hips, squeezing her as she continued to hump his erection through their clothes. It wasn't enough. He needed more of her. He needed all of her. He pulled back quickly and pulled his wallet from his trouser pocket as Kitty pulled herself up to a sitting position.

As Anthony opened his wallet and pulled out a foil packet, Kitty made quick work of releasing him from his trousers and yanking down his boxer shorts.

"Oh fuck, Kitty," Anthony growled as she took his length in her hand and began to massage back and forth. "Fuck, that feels so good."

Kitty massaged him harder and faster, and he felt his hips buck as she pleasured him with her hand. He had to get inside her. Now.

"I need you," he breathed. "I've needed you for so long."

"I need you too," Kitty whispered. "Fill me, Anthony, fill me now."

She pulled back from him, settling back onto her forearms as he pulled off her panties and ripped open the condom packet. He rolled on the condom and braced himself. He took hold of her thighs and pulled her to him, settling her thighs against his hips. Then finally, he slid a hand between them and guided himself as he slid past her hot wet folds and entered her.

The feeling of between inside Kitty's hot, wet, most intimate space was more than Anthony had dreamed. It was more than he ever realised he wanted. He couldn't find the words in his head as he mentally tried to place what he was feeling. He wanted more, needed more. He needed all of her. He pulled her closer still and thrust deeper into her.

Anthony looked down at Kitty and saw that she had her eyes tightly shut. He stilled, and her eyes sprung open.

"Are you alright, baby?" he asked anxiously.

"I'm close," she panted.

It was all Anthony needed to hear. He pulled back slightly and then thrust into her, deeply.

Kitty gasped and bucked hard against him, and it almost undid him. He thrust into her again, and she responded by bucking harder. Over and over, they danced this dance. She met every thrust as he gripped her hips, holding her against him.

He'd need this for so long. Anthony had waited a lifetime to feel what it would be like to be inside of Kitty. Now he knew he never wanted it to end. He knew that it would all be over between them once he climaxed, and he didn't want to let that happen. He focused his mind solely on her pleasure. He moved a hand, bringing it between her legs and began to work on rubbing that spot again. She groaned and wriggled and bucked, and he had to fight to keep from exploding.

He looked at her beautiful face. Her eyes were closed, and her mouth was open as she tipped her head back and moaned over and over. Her chocolate brown hair was splayed out across his desk, shining under the lamplight as she lay there, writhing against the pleasure he was bringing her. Then he felt it.

The first wild, clenching waves of Kitty's orgasm began, and she pressed harder against Anthony. She grabbed his hand and held it over her spot, encouraging him to rub harder as he pounded into her over and over. He watched as she bit her other hand to keep from screaming as her orgasm gripped her, and he knew he was close. He was really close.

The hot waves of her orgasm went on and on, pushing him closer to the edge as he thrust harder and faster inside her, still rubbing that most sensitive spot between her legs.

"Anthony,'" Kitty cried out as he rubbed her faster, penetrated her deeper. "Oh god, Anthony, please don't stop. Don't ever stop. I need you."

"Fuck, Kitty," Anthony growled. "Fuck I can't. I need..."

Suddenly Kitty grabbed his shoulders and pulled herself up and him down at the same time. Their bodies were pressed tightly together as her breasts rubbed against the cotton of his shirt. Still, she continued to explode around him, and Anthony felt her nails dig into his shoulders as she gripped him tightly, holding their bodies against each other.

"Oh god, Kitty," Anthony panted. "I need it. I need to come. I need it now."

"Yes, Anthony," Kitty cried out. "I need you to come. Come for me now."

Finally, as he pulled his arms around her, it happened. Holding her hard against him, Anthony thrust one last time and exploded into the condom he was wearing inside of her. He was lost. His mind was blank, and all he could feel was his pleasure, her pleasure, their pleasure. He spilt his hot load into the sheaf, still holding her, still pumping in a state of glorious ecstasy as he felt her orgasm begin to ebb away.

Anthony held Kitty in his arms, lost in the ecstasy of the pleasure they had shared. He cradled her in his arms and kissed her head softly, just needing to be close to her for a moment longer.

"I love you, Kitty," he whispered. "I love you so much."

Fifteen

Kitty's heart slammed against her chest and then halted as if she'd just done an emergency stop. *What the fuck did Anthony just say?* Surely that was all in her head. She'd imagined it, right? He didn't really say that? But he had. She knew he had.

A wave of nausea washed over her, and she felt dizzy as panic gripped her. Her fight or flight response suddenly became geared toward flight, and she wanted to run from the room as fast as she could.

She pushed Anthony away from her abruptly. He hadn't even pulled out of her, but she didn't care. The room was closing in on her, and she needed to get the hell away from him as soon as possible.

"Kitty?" he asked. "Are you alright?"

He tried to step closer to her, but she pushed him away before clamouring off the desk. She rolled her skirt back down and crossed her arms tightly across her chest, covering her breasts. She felt exposed, and she felt frightened. More frightened than she could put into words.

"No, I'm bloody not alright," she snapped. "Why would you say something like that?"

"Kitty, I wasn't expecting anything from you," he told her. "I told you because I didn't want you to leave without knowing the truth. Nothing more."
"Rubbish," she shot. "You said it to keep me here. Well, it won't work, Anthony. I will not be manipulated, and I will not be controlled."
She turned away from him and grabbed her discarded bra from the floor. She frantically began to pull it on over her boobs in a desperate bid to feel less vulnerable.
"That's not why I said it, and you know it," Anthony sighed.
"You can't," Kitty said. She could hear the trembling of her voice now, and she was certain Anthony could hear it too. "You can't love me, Anthony; you just can't."
"I'm not asking you for anything, Kitty," he insisted. "I know you're leaving. I just wanted you to know. I don't expect you to feel the same way."
"Good," she said firmly, pulling on her blouse. "Because I don't. And I don't want to talk about this anymore either."
"Kitty," he started, but she cut him off.
"No, Anthony," she hissed. "I don't want to talk about this. This was all a mistake, a foolish mistake."

Her hands trembled as she buttoned up her blouse, and it took her several attempts to keep the buttons in the loops. When she finally turned to face Anthony, he was his trousers on and his shirt tucked in. She wondered briefly if he was still wearing the condom under his clothes. He must have been; there was no way he'd have tossed it into the bin in his office.

As she looked at him, she could see the hurt evident on his face. *Shit.* She hadn't wanted to hurt him, but she just couldn't handle his feelings for her. She certainly couldn't tell him she felt the same way. As she scooped down to pick up her underwear and pull it on, she saw Anthony turn away from her. As she wrestled into her panties and fumbled her way through, reattaching her stockings to her suspender belt, she watched Anthony collect up the discarded paperwork off the floor. He made no effort to look at her as he crouched down, gathering up discarded pieces of paper.

Finally, she finger-combed her hair and tucked her blouse in. Then without saying another word, she walked quickly to the door, opened it and left Anthony in his office.

She felt the eyes of everyone she passed burning into her, her own eyes burning with tears. She stormed out of the building and headed over to her S.U.V. She leant against the side of the vehicle and tried to catch her breath as tears streamed down her cheeks.

Finally, she walked around to the passenger side door and opened it. She climbed in and sat in the passenger seat, thankful that she hadn't bothered to lock it while it was secure on school grounds. She could not have faced having to head into the meeting room and coming face-to-face with her team when she went to fetch her keys. She opened the glove box and pulled out her *only for when I'm really pissed off* cigarettes.

"Boy, am I pissed off!" she muttered.

In seven years, she'd never once argued with her kids' headteacher. Today, all they'd done was argue. Argue and struggle to keep their hands off of each other. She knew why, of course; it was just the tension and emotion of the situation. Nothing more.

She'd seen it all over the years. When people were hurting or frightened or grieving, they did all sorts of things they never usually did. They argued, they drank, they got into physical fights, or they shagged. Sometimes they did all of it. Her preferred method was to swim or at least see how long she could float face down in the water until she needed to come up for air.

Her behaviour today had been entirely out of character for her. She was sure it had been entirely out of character for Anthony too.

Anthony had told her, though, that he loved her. Did he mean it, or was he just confused by all the emotion of the day? And why had it caused her to panic so much?

Surely he was just feeling the confusion, the emotion and the trauma of the day. He didn't really love her. He just couldn't.

She heard footsteps approaching, and the driver's side door of the S.U.V. opened. She held out the packet of cigarettes.

"Weren't you remotely worried that I could have been coming to shoot you?" Peter asked as he climbed into the driver's seat.

"Not remotely," she shrugged. "I've been listening to the way you walk for two decades. I know your footsteps like I know my own."

"Fair enough," Peter said, taking a cigarette from the pack before handing the rest back to Kitty.

"I can't find my lighter," she said a little impatiently as she rummaged through the glove box.

"I've got one," Peter said. He put his hand in his trouser pocket and pulled out a yellow, disposable lighter. He lit his cigarette and then handed the lighter to Kitty.

She lit her cigarette, took a long pull, inhaled and then let out a long, sighing breath.

"What happened?" Peter asked, pulling on his own cigarette.

"He said he loves me," Kitty said, sighing once more.

"And that's a problem?" Peter asked.

Kitty rolled her eyes in frustration. "Of course, it's a bloody problem," she said impatiently.

"I thought you were going to tell me he was no good in bed," Peter said before putting the cigarette back to his lips.

"We never made it to a bed," Kitty confessed. "And he was bloody amazing, but that isn't the point."

"What is the point?" Peter asked.

Kitty took a long hard pull of her cigarette before answering.

"I'm leaving Peter," She said. "I can't get involved. I can't start something that I'm going to have to walk away from. I can't get into a relationship with my kids' headteacher. I can't...."

"Get your heart broken again," Peter finished for her.

She nodded as a single tear slipped down her cheek.

"He could have died today," she said as she quickly swiped at the tear with the back of her hand. "He could have died right there in the middle of the road, just like Jack."

"But he didn't," Peter said.

"He could have," Kitty pressed.

"Yes, and he could get into an accident on the motorway tomorrow," Peter reminded her.

"Which quite frankly is much more likely."

"That's not the point," Kitty said.

"What is the point?" Peter asked again as he inhaled on his cigarette.

Kitty stared out into the car park. There were armed police stationed at the gates, vehicles parked in random places and additional floodlighting set up to make the car park more visible in the night sky. Finally, she turned back to Peter and let out a long sigh.

"The point is Peter," Kitty said. "My job is dangerous. Now that my identity has been compromised, that puts a target on his back."

"Doesn't it make the girls targets too?" Peter asked.

"The girls and I can leave and start again somewhere else," she told him.

"Why can't Anthony?" he asked her.

Kitty looked at Peter like he'd grown two heads.

"Anthony's whole life is here," she reminded him. "I can't ask him to give all of that up."

"Can't or won't?" Peter pressed.

He was really starting to push her buttons. No doubt because over the years, he had been the only person she'd let get close enough to do it and get away with it. She was regretting that right now.

"I won't," she said simply. "I love Anthony, but-"

Did she really just say she loved him? It hit it here like a slap in the face. She loved him.

"There you go," Peter said. "It wasn't so hard for you to say once you let your guard down a little."

Before she could stop herself, Kitty burst into tears.

Peter flicked his cigarette into the drain next to where the S.U.V. was parked and took Kitty's hand. She didn't pull back. She just sat there, holding his hand as the tears fell.

"I can't do this again," she sobbed. "I can't love someone only to lose them again. I just can't."

"But you already love him," Peter said softly. "And if you run away now without giving him a chance, you'll be losing him anyway."

"But what if I do give him a chance and he dies too?" Kitty asked between sobs.

"There are no guarantees in this life, Kitty. After the breast cancer took Julie, I thought I would never love again," Peter said of the death of his first wife. "I made a vow to never get close to anyone again. But then Sarah came along, and slowly but surely, I let her into my heart. Oh, I fought it; you know I did. Eventually, though, I realised the only thing I was fighting was my second chance at happiness. Next month will be our tenth wedding anniversary, and I am so happy with her. She made me whole again."

Kitty nodded. She remembered all too well how awful it had been for Peter when he lost Julie. Yet, she remembered the look on his face when he stood at the altar next to Sarah as they exchanged their vows as well. He had been so happy that day and the look of love between them hadn't faded since.

He'd found a second chance at happiness, and he'd taken it. Maybe he was right. Perhaps she and Anthony could do it too.

She reached into the glove box once more and pulled out a packet of tissues. She let go of Peter's hand and opened the tissues. Laughing to herself, she wiped her eyes and blew her nose.

"I need to tell him," she said. "I need to tell Anthony that I love him."

"Yes, you do," Peter agreed. "But first, have another cigarette and let your eyes settle down. You look like you've just lost a boxing match with those puffy circles."

Kitty laughed, sniffed and lit another cigarette. "What do I do if he doesn't want me?" she asked earnestly. "What do I do if I am asking too much by asking him to come away with me? I was pretty horrible when he told me he loved me and all we've done today is argue."

"Today doesn't count," he said softly. "You've known this man for years, and I've never heard you say anything but good things about him. In fact, you've talked about him with such affection for so long, I've known for a long time that you loved him, even if you didn't. And I think he has known it too."

They sat in comfortable silence while they smoked their cigarettes. Then they got out of the S.U.V. and met at the tailgate.

"Go get your man," Peter said as Kitty finger-combed her hair and smoothed down her skirt.

"I will," She promised. "And this time, I won't let him go."

She hugged Peter tightly, giggled like a giddy school girl and headed inside.

Kitty walked slowly and deliberately to Anthony's office, keeping her breath slow and steady. She wanted to be calm when she saw him. She wanted to tell him she loved him in a moment of peace, not another argument.

As she reached his door, she knocked and took one last steadying breath before opening it.

Anthony was nowhere to be seen when she stepped into his office. The lights were on, but he wasn't there. Neither were the broken computer monitor pieces.

Kitty stepped back into the corridor and spoke to the officer guarding Anthony's office.

"Do you know where the headteacher went?" she asked.

The head hasn't left his office General," the female officer told her.

"Hmm," Kitty mused. "I'll check his private quarters."

Kitty headed back inside, closed the door and crossed the room. In the far right corner, there was a door. She knew from the school floor plans she had acquired that it led to his private residence. She knocked on the door. No answer. She went inside. The door opened into a large sitting area.

"You just love your brown leather," she mumbled as she went inside and looked around the room. Sure enough, a brown leather three-piece suite dominated the space. Anthony wasn't there, though. She checked his kitchen, his bedroom and his bathroom. She even checked his walk-in wardrobe. There was no sign of Anthony. She was about to head back out to the officer at the door to ask if she'd taken a break at any point, when she spotted it.

An envelope on the small writing desk in his living room.

Kitty crossed over to the desk and picked up the envelope.

It simply had *Kitty* written on the front of it.

She tore it open, her fingers trembling.

Dear Kitty,

I've gone to find my staff and students. I know you wanted me to wait and trust that you were close to finding them, but I need to do this. I need to see if they'll exchange at least the students for me. I'm valuable to them Kitty, they'll think they can get information out of me about your operation and about the high profile families at this school. If they think I am willing to give that up, maybe they'll give up the girls in return.

I don't know; I just know I have to try.

I'll never regret making love to you. I'll never regret being in love with you, and if I fail tonight, please know my last thoughts will be of you.

I love you, Kitty, and I know that deep down, you love me too.
Always yours.
Anthony.
Kitty screamed, her vision blurred, and she felt sick. She was shaking, coughing and heaving. Panic crippled her, and she felt like she was going to collapse. She tried to sink to the floor, but someone had hold of her arms. There was somebody there, holding her up. She blinked and looked around. She was still standing behind the S.U.V. with Peter. A vision. It had been a vision. "What did you see, Kitty?" Peter asked. "Kitty, tell me. What did you see?"
"He's gone," she choked. "Anthony's gone."
And with that, Kitty turned and threw up in the school car park.

Sixteen

Kitty stood there at the desk in Anthony's living room. Her entire body felt numb. She felt sick, and she felt broken. How could she not have seen this coming earlier? How could she not have realised that Anthony had been planning this all along? He had made it clear to her that he wanted to turn himself in and lead her to the hostages, but she thought she had convinced him it was a bad idea. Now he was missing, and she didn't know how to find him or if she would ever see him alive again. Her worst fears were coming to pass. Peter picked up the envelope, opened it and read the letter. "It's exactly as you said," he told her. Kitty nodded. She knew what the letter said. It was ingrained in her mind. It was etched into her memory as if someone had engraved it on stone. *I love you, Kitty, and I know that deep down, you love me too.*
The only thing was, she didn't want to love him. Not now, not at that moment; it hurt her too much.
"What the hell was he thinking?" Kate asked, coming to stand next to Kitty.
"He was thinking we aren't moving fast enough, and he was right," Kitty said.

"We're going as fast as we can, General," Kate said defensively.

"It's not fast enough," Kitty said. "I should have been out there searching. Not here having a shag on the headteacher's desk."

"You're not being fair to yourself, Kitty," Peter told her. "Your assigned role in this situation was to work with and support the headteacher because you know him better than anyone else on the team. And on a more personal note, your role was to be here with your daughters and the man you love. You were here, keeping your family safe."

Kate looked at Peter and then at Kitty. "You love him?" she asked softly.

Kitty nodded sadly.

"We'll get him back," Kate told her. "I promise you, we'll get him back."

Kitty just stood there. She was frozen. She didn't know what to say. She didn't know what to do.

All she knew was he was gone, likely going to be executed, and she hadn't told him how she felt. It was like Jack and the twins all over again.

Anthony was going to die alone, not knowing the truth.

How could she have been stupid enough to make the same mistake twice? How could she have left him alone like that? She should have stayed with him and faced her feelings instead of running away like some coward and leaving him to go after a dangerous group of terrorists himself.

It didn't seem real to Kitty. None of it. Her and Anthony finally admitting they had feelings for each other. Kissing in the classroom. Anthony getting shot. Them making love in his office. Him telling her that he loved her. Her running away. Him going missing.

Kitty replayed all of it in her mind. It all felt like a terrible dream, and she couldn't accept that this was the reality of the situation. She couldn't accept the fact that she might never see him alive again.

Kitty became aware of her feet moving but didn't know how. Then she realised, she was sitting in the leather armchair in Anthony's living room. "She's in shock," she heard Peter say. "Get a medic in here, and whatever you do, don't let her girls hear about this."

Kitty just sat there, staring blankly at the dark stained hardwood floor, desperately trying to see something. She replayed the vision in her mind over and over, looking for anything she had missed. Trying to see any clue Anthony might have left. There had to be something she was missing, one small detail. Something, anything that would help her piece all of this mess together.

And that's when it hit her.

Kitty scrambled to her feet, and yelled, "Someone get my tactical gear, right now."

She barged past Peter and rushed into Anthony's bedroom. She crossed the room and pulled open the walk-in wardrobe door.

That's when she saw it. Everything had all been shoved to one side in the wardrobe.

Peter followed her.

"Kitty?" he asked, clearly puzzled.

"Look," Kitty said as she looked at the clothes handing in the built-in cupboard. "Does Anthony strike you as the kind of man who would just have all his clothes carelessly shoved to one side in his wardrobe like this? Would he leave his pristine shirts and suits, all bunched together like this?"

"Actually, no," Peter said.

"And look at the way his clothes are set out," Kitty continued. "There's no way someone, as organised as Anthony, would have all of his clothes shoved over to that side where he'd have to pick them with his right hand. He's left-handed and far too efficient to make things harder on himself like that. There's something here."

Kate arrived with an Army doctor and a soldier carrying her tactical kit.

General Kline," the doctor said. "I'd like a moment of your time, please."

"I'd like a moment to give you Doc," she said. "However, I don't have one right now."

"General," Kate said softly. "You really do need to see the doctor."

"Like fuck I do," Kitty snapped as she barged past everyone and took her tactical kit from the young soldier holding it.

She turned back to Peter. "I need to change," she told him. "You keep looking and tell me what you see. Then gear up. We're heading out."

"General Kline," the doctor said more firmly. "If you do not stop what you're doing right now and engage with me, I am afraid I will have to declare you unfit for duty."

Kitty felt her frustration levels rise, and she turned to face the doctor. Her mood must have been written all over her face because he took one look at her expression and stepped back. She didn't have time for this shit.

"Listen up, Doc," She said sharply. "I was not in shock; I was meditating."

"Meditating?" he asked.

"Yes, meditating," she said. "I shut myself off from all external factors so that I could look within, replay the vision and look to see what I had missed. It's like rewinding a film. You know when you turn away from the screen to pick up your drink, only for something good to happen? You go back to see what you've missed, right? Well, sometimes if I am very quiet and very still and I focus really hard, I can do that with my visions."

"Bingo."

The sound came from the wardrobe.

"Peter?" she called as she made her way back to where she'd left him just moments ago.

"You were exactly right General, there is something here," he said. "It took me a moment to spot it, but there's a carefully concealed panel. It leads down a flight of stairs and into a tunnel."

"Peter, you are a fucking legend," Kitty told her old friend.

She turned back to Kate and said, "No one enters that wardrobe without my express permission."

"Yes, Ma'am," Kate said as she stood to attention and saluted.

"Walters," Kitty said as she turned her attention to the doctor. "You have tactical training and have seen active duty on the front lines, yes?"

"Yes, General," he confirmed.

"Then providing you think I'm fit for duty, gear up. You're coming with me."

"Yes, Sir," he called as he too stood to attention and saluted before heading out of the room.

"Major Lee," she said, turning to Peter.

"Ma'am," he responded, suddenly standing much taller.

"Oh behalf of Her Majesty the Queen and with the authority of my role as General of the British Army, I hereby recall you to active duty and promote you to the rank of Colonel. And if you salute me, I will shoot you. Do you understand and accept this recall and promotion of your own free will?"

"Yes, General", he said, and Kitty could see he was desperate to salute her.

"I'm warning you, Peter," she said. "Do not do it."

"Yes, Ma'am," Peter said, smirking.

She rolled her eyes and turned her attention to the soldier who had brought in her tactical gear.

"Private Thorpe," she said quickly.

"Yes, General," he answered, standing to attention.

"Tactical gear for yourself and Colonel Lee, please. We move out in five minutes."

When Peter and Thorpe had left the room, and they were alone, Kitty turned to Kate as she began to change into her tactical gear.

"I need you on this mission, Kate," she said.

"General, I can't," Kate said quickly as she stepped back.

"Hey," Kitty said. "There are no ranks here right now. This is just us. Sister witches and friends."

"Please don't order me to come on this mission Kitty," Kate said. "I'm just not ready."

"You're never going to be ready, Kate, but you've been behind a desk for a year, and now I need you. I'm not going to order you, but I am asking you, sister. Please stand with me. I need you."

Kate nodded slowly.

"That's my girl," Kitty said as she began to check the contents of her vest. "Don't worry, I've got your back, and I know you've been practising every single day. What happened during Operation Castle Down won't happen again. I believe in you. I know you can…."

She stopped in her tracks and turned to face Kate. "Kit?" Kate asked.

"My homing beacon isn't here," Kitty said as she began emptying out her pockets, throwing the contents onto Anthony's bed.

"That's odd," Kate said. "Where did you last have it?"

"It was tucked into my stocking," she said. "Oh my god."

She ran from the room, in only her cargo trousers, bra, socks and boots. She ran right through the living room and into Anthony's office, stopping in front of his desk and turning her attention to the hardwood floor.

"Here," she told Kate. "We had sex right here."

"Too much information, but thanks," Kate said.

"No," Kitty said. "You don't get it. We were right here, and he ran his hands down my thighs before putting his hand in his pocket to grab a condom from his wallet."

"Well, I'm glad you were safe," Peter said as he entered the room.

"You're not paying attention," Kitty yelled excitedly. "He took it. Anthony has my beacon."

"Whoa," Peter mused. "You mean to tell me that he had sex with you just to get his hands on your equipment?"

"I'm not sure that's what you meant to say actually, Pete," Kate said, smirking.

"Oh, will you all just stop fucking around and get ready?" Kitty yelled, running back the way she'd come so that she could finish getting ready.

"Kit, where are you going?" Peter called after her.

"To finish gearing up," she yelled. "We now know how to find Anthony and hopefully everyone else too."

Kitty ran back to the bedroom and finished getting dressed. She shoved her hair into a low ponytail and secured her tactical vest. Then she paused and looked around the room.

This was Anthony's bedroom. The place where he dressed, where he slept and where he watched T.V. in bed. Since everyone else was gearing up, she had a few moments to herself where she could spend a little time in silence, feeling close to Anthony.

She sat down on his bed. Of course, it was mahogany and perfectly neat and tidy.

"You're such a goth," she whispered as she ran her hand over the smooth cotton duvet cover. It was a deep shade of red with a black trim. His pillowcases were the opposite, black with a red trim. She picked up one of the pillows, pulled it toward her and wrapped her arms around it. As she cuddled the pillow, she inhaled deeply, drinking in Anthony's scent. She could smell his aftershave and could feel him in the room with her.

Tears welled in her eyes, and she hugged the pillow tighter, not wanting to let it go, but she felt something inside the pillowcase. She slipped her hand inside, felt around and pulled out what felt like an unframed photo. She studied it carefully. It was a photo of her and Anthony standing at the mulled wine stall at the school Christmas Fayre last year.

They'd been having a casual debate about mulled wine versus snowballs, and someone on the P.T.A. had snapped a photo of them. She hadn't even noticed it was being taken. They had both been too busy laughing together to notice the camera. The first time Kitty had seen the photo was when it appeared on the school website. She'd saved it to her personal phone and looked at it most days.

She'd thought she was crazy, but it turned out Anthony had liked it so much that he'd printed it and kept it close by. He'd kept her close by.

"Oh, Ant," she sighed as she tucked the picture back inside his pillowcase and set the pillow down. "I'm coming for you, baby, I promise." She stood and moved over to the tall mahogany chest of drawers in the corner of Anthony's bedroom. She picked up the bottle of aftershave he had sitting on top and took off the lid. She held it close to her with both hands and sniffed the spray nozzle. She loved that smell. It reminded her of him, and it made her feel safe. It made her feel close to him and gave her the courage and the motivation she needed to get out there and find him.

She sprayed a little on her neck and her wrists before putting the lid back on and setting it back down on the chest of drawers.

"There," she said quietly. "Now I'm carrying you with me."

She turned around and froze. Kate, Peter, Walters, and Thorpe were all standing in the doorway of Anthony's bedroom. She'd had her back to the door for so long that she had no idea how long they had been there.

"I have a new homing beacon for you, General," Kate said as she stepped forward.

Kitty met Kate in the middle of the room and took the homing beacon from her open palm.

"Smells good," Kate said as she sniffed Kitty lightly.

Kitty nodded and smiled slightly.

"Come on," Kate said. "Let's go get your man."

"Into Narnia," Kitty said, and she led the way to Anthony's wardrobe.

Seventeen

Anthony's head throbbed, his body hurt, and his eyes stung. He was exhausted, and he felt sick. He'd taken quite the beating when he'd been picked up by S.W.O. before they'd thrown him into the boot of their car. He hadn't had time to register the make and model, but he knew something. It wasn't designed for a man of six feet four inches.

He felt cramped and claustrophobic, mostly though, he felt determined. He was going to get his students to safety, even if it killed him. He knew it probably would.

He hadn't made any effort to fight back when he'd been captured. He hadn't resisted or tried to defend himself when he'd been beaten.

He felt the car come to a stop and the engine shut off. They'd arrived. Shifting so that his hands could reach his ankle, he quickly reached into his sock and made a grab for the homing beacon he'd stashed in there. He pushed it down further into his sock, ensuring it was secure, but he didn't activate it. He wouldn't activate it until he was sure he was in the right place and had seen his missing friends and students with his own eyes.

In the meantime, he had left Kitty another gift at his abduction site. Once that would lead her in the right direction until he was sure it was safe to activate the homing beacon.

He heard the car doors open and felt them slam closed, the action causing pain to tear through him. The car's boot popped open, and before he had the chance to think, he was pulled from the vehicle.

The hood over his face kept him from seeing anything, but he knew there were two gunmen. He didn't resist. He knew they wouldn't shoot him as neither man had the voice from the video. That man was the one who wanted to kill him. He wanted to do it personally.

It hadn't stopped these two clowns from giving him a good beating, but that worked for him. It meant he was able to provide Kitty with precisely what she needed to start the search process.

He'd been punched in the face, kicked in the stomach, taken a rounders bat to the back of the knees and had been slashed in the arm with a penknife, causing his stitches to rip open. If truth be told, he was in agony, but it was worth it for the fresh blood he had left at the scene. Blood he knew Kitty could now use to track him.

As the gunmen grabbed his elbows and pulled him, he walked with them willingly. They walked across what felt like damp grass under his trainers and into what he assumed was the warehouse. The overwhelming stench of fish nauseated him, and he had to fight the urge to be sick. He was definitely in the right place. As soon as he could be sure everyone else was still here, he'd find a way to activate the homing beacon and let Kitty know precisely where he was.

As Anthony was dragged through the building, he could hear the ever-increasing sound of sobs until he heard a door open, and he was pushed into a room. The hood was pulled off of his head, and he was shoved to the floor.

"Good news, Bruv," one of the gunmen said. "You get to see these pretty faces one last time before our boss shanks you." Then both gunmen left, shutting the door behind them.

Kitty had given Kate the keys to her S.U.V. and told her to gather their team and be on standby. She had taken Peter, Thorpe and Walters with her into the secret passageway that led out of Anthony's built-in wardrobe.

As they walked, Kitty pondered the hidden exit and why it wasn't on the floorplans for the school. She supposed one of the headteachers from years past had it installed, but which one? That building had been a school for more than one hundred and fifty years. It had been built during Queen Victoria's reign for the elite families. The ones who had been wealthy enough to send their kids to school rather than to the workhouses.

It took Kitty and her team about ten minutes to make their way through the dark passage, with only torchlight to guide them. Nothing of consequence had captured their attention before the tunnel finally brought them to a dead end. A ladder leading up to a manhole cover brought them out into a meadow well beyond the school's boundary. They each climbed the ladder in turn, Kitty in front and Peter bringing up the rear.

The group carefully followed where Anthony had been with torches, using the freshly flattened down flowers from his footsteps as a guide. Then, finally, they reached the roadside. Kitty wasn't sure which direction they should head for a moment, but then she spotted a small blue chalk-drawn arrow on the ground.

"Good boy Anthony," Kitty said as she hurried forward in the direction the arrow was pointing to. Considering this was all so new to Anthony, he knew exactly what he had been doing when he set off, and he had gone out of his way to make it easy for Kitty to trace him.

Kitty looked at the tablet she was holding in her hand, checking the tracking app. She'd set it to look for the homing beacon Anthony had taken, but as of yet, there was no alert. He hadn't had the chance to activate it yet. Maybe whoever had taken him had found it and tossed it.

She didn't believe that, though, not really. She knew Anthony would have concealed it well enough that it wouldn't have been easy to find if he'd been searched. It was more likely he didn't want to activate it until he had been delivered to the warehouse.

Kitty followed the path until it reached a main crossroads.

"Quick," she said to her team. "Everyone look for a blue chalk arrow."

"There," Peter called, and they crossed the road in the direction Anthony had gone.

As they got to the other side of the road, another chalk line indicated that he had opted to turn right, so they sped up, breaking into a jog. Then finally, Kitty had seen it. A piece of blue chalk broken up and trodden into the pavement.

"Here," she said as she crouched down to look at the crushed chalk. "This is where Anthony was taken."

She pressed her new homing beacon, alerting Kate of her location and signalling that she was ready for the rest of her team to arrive.

"Where do you think they took him?" Peter asked.

"God knows," Kitty sighed as she began to search the ground around her.

"What are you looking for?" Peter asked her.

"My old homing beacon," she said. "If Anthony's as clever as I think he is, he wouldn't have put it in his pocket. But if they searched him and found it, they would have tossed it out before driving off."

The three men with Kitty began to search for the beacon as well. Each carefully looking with their torches.

"We need more light, Kit," Peter called from the other side of the road.

"On it," Kitty called back.

She walked into the middle of the road and stood there. She stood tall with her feet wide and her hands down by her sides, palms up. She focused, and silently she called upon the element of fire. Kitty felt her hands getting hot, so she closed her eyes and lifted her head up to the sky. Slowly she drew her arms up above her head. Light shone from her hands, and then very quickly, she dropped to her knees and brought her hands down, slapping them onto the tarmac of the road. The road around Kitty lit up in a white, glowing light as if the ground itself was now one massive torch.

"Holy shit," Thorpe exclaimed.

Kitty painted on her hands and knees on the ground, and Walters rushed over to her, kneeling by her side.

"I'm alright," she assured him. "Magic like that allows for a lot of energy to flow through me, and it knocks me on my arse, but I'm alright."

"You sure?" Walters asked as he handed her a pouch of water from his med kit.

Kitty nodded and took the pouch, tearing it open. "Keep looking," she said before gulping down the cool water.

She sat and rested for a few moments, catching her breath and grounding herself. Her palms down on the ground, she allowed herself to draw in the neutral energy of the earth. In an ideal situation, she would have cast a protective circle and grounded herself before performing spells that required her to call in that much energy from the elements. This situation, though, was anything but ideal.

"I really don't think the beacon is here, Kitty," Peter said as he crouched down next to her.

"Good," Kitty said. Then there's a good chance Anthony still has it.

"I have to tell you something, though," Peter said.

"You found blood," Kitty said.

"I'm afraid so," Peter confirmed.

"That's brilliant," Kitty said excitedly as she scrambled to her feet.

"Did I miss something?" Peter asked.

Kitty didn't answer, but rushed over to where Thorpe and Walters were standing. She looked down at the blood.

"There's not enough for me to be concerned," Walters said.

"It's enough," Kitty said. "And it's fantastic."

"Are you feeling better?" Walters asked.

Clearly, he was confused about what had Kitty so excited. He probably thought it was a side effect of the spell she had just cast.

"Much," she said as she turned away from the blood pool and brushed the dirt off her trousers. "Just needed a little grounding."

"Magic and Medicine," Walters groaned. "They just shouldn't mix."

As Thorpe approached them, Kitty checked the time on her watch. 23:54 hours.

Kitty estimated that Anthony had been gone for a little over an hour. She had a plan of action now. All she needed was some help to get it in motion. She saw the flashing of red and blue lights in the distance, and she knew her team was close.

She crouched down to where the small pool of blood lay in the road. Anthony's blood. Peter, Walters and Thorpe stepped away from Kitty, giving her some space. They probably thought she was going to have a meltdown or something. She didn't

This time Anthony's blood didn't distress her. It didn't bring back the traumatic memory of Uncle Tim's death. This time it excited her. She needed Anthony's blood to track him and the hostages. Since she couldn't get his location using the homing beacon, she and her coven would track them with a fresh spill like this.

Several vehicles pulled up at the scene, and Kate climbed out of Kitty's car. Behind that was another S.U.V. that Kitty knew had the over five principal members of her team. The other five members of her coven. They, too, climbed out of their S.U.V.

Now Kitty had everyone she needed for a blood to blood spell.

They joined where she stood over Anthony's blood.

"It's a bit bright out here, Kit," Kate said. "I bet that knocked you on your arse."

"Just a bit," Kitty admitted.

"Did you at least ground yourself?"

"Did she fuck?" Peter said, coming to stand with the group.

"She did ground after though," Walters said as he too joined Kitty and her coven.

Thorpe also joined them. Together the ten of them stood there for a moment. They looked down at the ground where Anthony's blood was puddled in the middle of the road.

Kitty looked at her watch again. 23:58.

"Right," she said firmly. "Kate, Si, Mark, Lisa, Dan, Chloe, let's do this."

She turned to face her team and gave them a double thumbs up. In just a few minutes, they would have an accurate way of tracking Anthony. Hopefully, that would lead them to the hostages as well.

"Do what?" Walters asked.

"A blood to blood spell," Chloe, one of Kitty's team and a member of her coven, answered.

"Basically, we are going to use Anthony's blood to direct us to him," Dan, another witch in Kitty's team, said.

"Sort of a supernatural compass," Kate added.

Kitty turned to Peter, Walters and Thorpe. "I need you all to stand right back so that when we begin, your energies are out of reach and don't mix with ours. Sorry."

"You heard her chaps," Peter said, and he, Thorpe and Walters went to stand where a crowd of police and soldiers were gathering by Kitty's S.U.V.

Kitty and the other six witches in her coven sat down on the ground in a circle and crossed their legs around Anthony's blood.

Her watch beeped. Midnight. The witching hour. Without needing any further instruction, the group began to cast a circle, chanting together.

"Guardians of the East, keepers of air, we summon you and ask you to be with us and protect us in this sacred space.

"Guardians of the south, keepers of the fire, we summon you and ask you to be with us and protect us in this sacred space.

"Guardians of the west, keepers of earth, we summon you and ask you to be with us and protect us in this sacred space.

"Guardians of the North, keepers of water, we summon you and ask you to be with us and protect us in this sacred space.

"Gods, goddesses, deities, angels and light beings, keepers of spirit, we summon you and ask you to be with us and protect us in this sacred space.

"So mote it be."

Kitty and her coven all placed their hands on the ground in front of them and closed their eyes. Silently they sat as they grounded themselves, pulling energy from the earth below them; imagining routes growing from their hands into the earth, drawing in clean, neutral energy. They all sat in complete silence for around two minutes. They allowed this process to happen naturally, not forcing it or rushing it.

Kitty was desperate to get into her S.U.V. and get moving, but she knew that they needed to be fully grounded, focused, and prepared for this spell to work. And she needed for this spell to work.

There were fourteen lives at risk, and finally, they had their first blood sample to work with. If they wasted this opportunity, they would have to go back to checking individual warehouses along the coast.

Kitty drew in a deep breath and exhaled loudly, opening her eyes. This was how each member of the coven signified they were ready when grounding themselves, and one by one, the others followed suit.

Finally, they were ready to cast.

Kitty took a steadying breath and began to recite a spell as the words formed in her heart.

"At midnight in the witching hour, we call upon these scared powers. We call to us the blood of Anthony so that we may find him and set him free. I call my lover back to me so that together we'll always be blessed be. We use this blood to track this man and ask it to roll to this here clan."

Kitty was impressed. She didn't like to make up the words for spells as she went along, but she wanted something more substantial than the regular blood to blood spell they would typically use. She wanted something personal and meaningful to add strength to the spell.

By itself, the pool of blood began to separate from one puddle into seven. Each little puddle rolled into a ball, and the balls rolled to each of the coven members. Its consistency changed to that of a toy marble, and each member picked up their new little blood ball. As they did, they felt them wriggle and pull slightly in their hands. Each one was pulling the same way, the direction Anthony had been taken.

The spell wouldn't last for long, but hopefully, it would last long enough for Anthony to activate the homing beacon.

They released the circle to safely expel the magical energy they had created and scrambled to their feet. It was go time.

Kitty clapped her hands twice and the road instantly became dark again.

"Keys," she called as she ran to her S.U.V.

"Still in the ignition," Kate called back.

Kitty climbed into the driver's seat, and Kate climbed into the middle seat in the back. Thorpe and Walters got in either side of Kate, and Peter got into the front passenger seat. The doors were closed, seatbelts were put on, and the ignition was started.

"Right," Kitty said as she slid the car from park and into drive and pulled away. "Let's go save some lives."

Eighteen

"Anthony," Clare exclaimed.
Anthony recognised Clare's voice instantly.
Relief washed over him. She sounded O.K.
He tried to open his eyes, but he couldn't focus.
His face was swollen, and he'd been in the dark
for too long. He stopped trying, accepting that he
would need some time to adjust to being back in
the light.
Anthony heard Clare shuffle over to him and felt
her use her hands to lift his head off of the floor
and onto her lap.
"Mr Richmond," several of the girls exclaimed at
once as gasps filled the cold, rancid air.
"The girls," he said to Clare.
"They're unharmed," Clare confirmed.
"Frightened, dirty and fed up with weeing in a
stinking bucket, but they are unharmed."
"It's good to hear your voices, girls," he called to
the group of teenagers who were somewhere in
the room.

He wished he could get his damned eyes to open and focus. He wanted to look at the girls and see for himself that they weren't injured. He wanted to see how they were coping and offer them some reassurance that everything would be alright. For now, though, he had no choice but to lay with his head on Clare's lap as she checked out his injuries.

"How's Bo doing?" Clare asked.

"Bo's O.K," Anthony assured her. "She misses her mum, but she's O.K. Chris and your parents are at the school with her; they're waiting for you."

A sob escaped Clare and Anthony lifted a hand to her. She took it, and he squeezed hers gently.

"You are going to get home to your daughter and your husband Clare, I promise," he whispered.

"She won't sleep without her special blankie," Clare choked.

"A grubby old pink thing with flowers on it?" Anthony asked.

"Yes," Clare exclaimed. "She has it?"

"Chris brought it to school with him," he said. "When we invited families to stay on-site, Chris picked up some bits for Bo on his way in."

"Oh god," Clare laughed. "She's going to have a skirt, odd socks and wellies."

"Well, that's not school uniform," Anthony teased. "We can't have that. We'd better get you home quickly before Chris lowers our standards."

"I'd like that very much," Clare sniffed. "I'm ready to leave here now."

"Soon," he told her. "I promise."

Anthony tried again to open his eyes, and his vision slowly began to come into focus. The room was bright. Too bright after being in the blacked-out boot of a car with a hood over his head. Finally, he looked around. The room was dirty and smelly. There were two buckets over in the far right corner, the floor was littered with what looked like rat droppings, and in the near right corner, a group of filthy, tear-stained teenagers looked at him. In the middle of the room, he saw a discarded pile of disposable plastic water bottles.

"You've been given water?" he asked as she forced himself to sit up.

"Yes, they've been quite forceful about making us drink," Clare told him. "I think the idea is, the more we drink, the more we pee and the more we pee, the worse the smell gets in here."

"Not to mention, the more humiliated everyone gets from having to pee in front of each other," Jenny said from across the room. "Psychological torture."

Anthony looked in the direction Jenny's voice had come from and saw that she was cradling Fitz. He was so severely beaten he was hardly recognisable. They were tucked up in the nearside left-hand corner of the room, away from everyone else. Jenny's back was turned slightly to the students at the other side of the room, and Anthony realised she had been trying to keep the girls from seeing what state Fitz was really in.

"How is he?" Anthony asked as he gently squeezed Clare's hand before releasing it again

"I think he has internal bleeding," Jenny said. "He's certainly got some broken bones and has been drifting in and out of consciousness for the past couple of hours."

Anthony shuffled over to where Fitz's broken and battered body lay on the ground, his head on Jenny's lap.

"Fitz," he called gently. "Fitz, can you hear me?"

There was no response. Fitz was in a bad way and needed to get to a hospital as soon as possible.

"Oh Kitty, you had better get here soon," Anthony muttered.

"Kitty?" Clare asked. "Kitty Kline? What exactly do you expect her to do about all of this?"

Anthony shuffled back until he was facing the entire group, almost like he was going to give an assembly.

"It turns out Ivy and Rosie's mum wasn't exactly honest with us about her true identity," he said, addressing everyone in the room. "Kitty is, in actual fact, a British Army General and leads a joint MI5-MoD taskforce."

He had purposely spoken as loudly as he could without shouting, knowing his captures would be listening. He needed them to think he had valuable information. It might be what kept the attention on him and off of the girls long enough for Kitty to get to them before the deadline.

"No kidding," Jenny said, shocked.

"I knew there was more to Kitty than meets the eye, Clare told Anthony. "I told you there was more to Kitty than you realised."

Anthony nodded and shuffled over to the group of terrified looking teenage girls. They were filthy, and they looked exhausted, their eyes swollen from crying. Yet, as he approached them, they each began to smile. They had hopeful expressions on their faces, and he knew they wanted him to give them something positive to hold on to. He knew he would have to do his best to come through for them, even if he was only able to offer them the tiniest glimmer of hope.

"Come closer, girls," he said, and the group crawled over to him and huddled as close as they possibly could.

"So," he said, smiling. "You won the netball match, eh?"

The group nodded, and some murmured little bits about their victory.

"I'm really proud of you girls," he said, smiling warmly. "You are champions, and you are fighters. I know you must all be terrified right now, but I want you all to know you've been remarkably brave."

He lowered his voice as much as he could, not wanting any guards outside the door to hear him. "You only have to be brave for a little while longer," he told the group. "You're going to get home to your parents before the night is through, and you're going to be safe again. Your families are waiting for you at school, and you'll be going home to them soon. Do you understand?"

One by one, each of the girls nodded and said that they understood.

"Do you remember the S.H.P. victory song?"

The girls nodded again.

"I need you to sing it for me now."

"You want us to sing?" one of the girls asked.

"Yes, and when you've done three rounds of that, sing something else. And sing loudly," he told them.

The girls began to sing.

"Good girls," he said as he smiled again. "Keep singing for me. I promise you; you are going home."

As the girls sang, Anthony shuffled back over to Clare, Jenny and a still unconscious Fitz. He knew he didn't have long, and he had a lot to tell them.

Kitty looked in her rear-view mirror. A disco of red and blue lights flashed behind her as she was followed by a motorcade of police and military vehicles as she pulled onto the dual carriageway. The road was quiet, which made it easier for Kitty. She was able to pull into the outside lane and put her foot down. Ninety miles an hour still seemed too slow, though. It felt as though she was driving in slow motion. She knew it would be unwise to go any faster, though, so she pressed the little button on her steering wheel, and the adaptive cruise control kicked in.

She needed to find Anthony before the spell crapped out if she was going to get to him and the hostages and rescue them. She contemplated speeding up a little more, but she knew it would be dangerous to drive any faster than she already was. She couldn't be careless, not when there were fourteen lives at stake and four passengers in the SUV with her.

"I need an update, Kate," Kitty said as she kept her attention focused on the road in front of her.

"Police in Sussex have raided thirty-one warehouses associated with fishing since we put the call out. They are either used in the catching, cleaning, preparation or storage for fish or have connections to fishing boats. They are continuing to search through the night with the assistance of Army personnel. There was some concern that Sussex might not have been the right direction, but given the time between the abduction and your second vision, it was the most likely scenario."

Kitty opened her palm slightly and looked down briefly at the blood ball dancing furiously within it.

"Judging by this, Sussex is definitely the right direction," she said as she quickly turned her attention back to the road. "I'd sure feel better if we had a more definitive direction, though."

"You and me both," Kate agreed.

They continued driving for about another twenty-five minutes. No one spoke during that time, and the space in the car was filled only by the sound of breathing.

"I can't stand this," Kitty muttered as she sped along the dual carriageway. "The silence is killing me.

"I know," Peter said. "Me too."

She glanced over at him quickly, and he patted her arm gently as a small laugh escaped her.

"Would you please put something on to listen to?" Kitty asked as she rolled her shoulders a few times. "I've got to release some of this tension on my back, neck and shoulders and clear my head."

"Any preference?" Peter asked as he loaded the media player in the car.

"There's a flash drive in the glove box," she said. "It's labelled Best Classics and has a bit of an eclectic selection on it. The smaller looking glove box thingy is a CD player, but it also has an SD card slot and a USB port. If you open it, you'll see."

Peter rummaged through the glove box and looked for the flash drive.

Ah-ah," he exclaimed as he held up the correct one.

"That's the one," Kitty said.

"What do you mean by best classics?" Peter asked, connecting the flash drive to the entertainment system.

"You know," Kitty said. "Handel, Schubert, Mozart, Tchaikovsky, Bach, Chopin. A collection of my favourite pieces from each composer.

"Don't you have anything with more life in it?" Peter asked.

"More life?" Kitty asked.

"As in people who lived in the last century."

"Oh," Kitty said. "No, not really. Well, not on that flash drive anyway."

"Alright," Peter submitted. "Which musical genius would you like to hear first?"

"Surprise me," Kitty instructed.

"As you wish," Peter said.

Kitty kept her eyes on the road as Peter selected a piece of music from the playlist that had appeared on the entertainment system's screen. The music began to play.

"Hmm," Kitty said, not taking her eyes off the road. "I'm not sure Tchaikovsky's Symphony Number Four in F Minor is going to going to do anything to settle the tension and anxiety I'm feeling."

"You peeked," Peter mock gasped.

"I did not," Kitty shot at him. "I just happen to listen to this when I am angry running."

"Angry running?" Peter asked.

"Yes," Kitty said. "Angry running. You know when someone really fucking annoys you, and so you go for a run to clear head."

"Ah, yes," Peter agreed. "You've had me doing many angry runs over the years."

"Fuck off," Kitty laughed.

The truth was, though, she could do with a good, angry run right now. There was nothing like the feeling of her trainer-clad feet pounding the pavements when she was feeling worked up and stressed out. Music in her ears, her heart pounding in her chest, and time to work through whatever issue was bothering her always did her good. Afterwards, she would feel calm and balanced again. And hungry. Her runs always ended with her going home and tucking into a banana split, even at eight in the morning.

Peter pressed the button on the entertainment system to skip to the next track.

"That's better," Kitty said as Bach's Cello Suite Number One in G Major began to play.

"Oh god," Peter groaned. "Just throw me out here, would you? I'd rather walk than listen to this shit."

"Shut the fuck up," Kitty said. Then she glanced briefly at Peter, saw his facial expression, turned her eyes back on to the road and burst out laughing. Before she knew it, everyone in the vehicle was laughing, and Kitty finally felt herself begin to relax.

Then she felt something in her hand, and all too quickly, her smile faded, and she stopped laughing.

Anthony pulled the homing beacon out of his sock and studied it briefly before he finally activated it. Now Kitty and her team would finally know exactly where he was and where the hostages were as well. They'd be getting out of here in no time. Then they could get Fitz to the hospital, and everyone else would finally be able to go home to their loved ones.

"Listen to me," Anthony whispered urgently, as he tucked the small gadget back into his sock and turned his attention to Jenny and Clare. "I'm not sure how long we have before the guards come in here and demand that the girls stop singing, and I want to talk to you without when hearing."

Clare and Jenny nodded.

"I got myself captured on purpose," he told them quickly. "There's a hidden passage that leads from the headteacher's quarters out of school grounds. The information has been passed down from head to head over the years, and I was the only one at school who knew about it or how to access it. Kitty has a homing beacon that she might have… erm… misplaced in my office. I took it, snuck out through the passageway with it and went for a run, knowing this lot wanted me." He motioned toward the door with a wave of his hand.

"That was very brave," Jenny said.

"Brave and stupid," Clare scolded, yet her expression was soft, and Anthony knew she wasn't being unkind.

"Just now, I activated the homing beacon," he continued. "Kitty and her team are on their way here right now."

Or at least he hoped they would be. He hoped Kitty had received his note by now and discovered that he had gone with her homing beacon. It must have been well over two hours since she'd stormed out of his office after they had made love.

"You have a lot of faith in Kitty," Jenny said. The questioning look in her eyes did not go unnoticed by Anthony.

"You would do too after seeing her today," he said. "She's amazing. She commands this entire task force, abseils from helicopters and carries guns and knives, the whole nine yards. Oh, and the witch stuff, completely real. Kitty gets these visions, and she knew you were in a warehouse that stank of fish. Her team have been searching warehouses across the coast for hours. Who knew there'd be so many of them, though?"

He was rambling. He was actually rambling. Him! He never rambled. He'd had years of training at speaking publicly as a headteacher. He knew how to hold an audience, and it sure as hell wasn't by babbling on like some crazy drunk.

He saw the look that passed between Jenny and Clare.

"What?" he asked.

They looked as they knew some sort of secret that he wasn't in the loop about.

"Oh, come on," Clare said. "Do you think the entire staff hasn't noticed over the years that you're head over heels in love with Kitty?"

"We've all seen it," Jenny confirmed. "You're nuts about her, no matter how much you try to pretend otherwise."

"The entire staff knows that I'm in love with Kitty?" he asked, frowning.

What the hell? Had it been a source of gossip between them? How had they all known when he hadn't even realised it himself?

"Well, I didn't know I was in love with her," he whispered furiously. "I only just figured it out tonight. Someone could have told me."

"We figured you'd realise eventually," Clare shrugged.

"We just never realised you'd be this slow," Jenny added.

"The Board of Governors are going to kill me," he sighed.

"The Board of Governors are going to have a parade," Clare said.

"They've known for ages," Jenny confirmed. "They've been taking bets on how much longer you were going to continue to make yourself miserable by living in denial."

"I've not been living in denial," Anthony said defensively. "I've been trying not to get the sack."

"Well, as a Staff Governor, I can tell you that you're not going to get the sack," Clare assured him. "We've been rooting for you two for years and we already have an agreement in writing that states if you ever came to your senses and hooked up with Kitty, you'd be allowed to keep your job."

"What?" Anthony asked. "Why?"

The rules on headteachers and parents were very clear in schools across the country. It wasn't respectable, and it wasn't allowed. More than once, he'd heard of headteachers being dismissed from their posts for inappropriate conduct with parents. What made his situation so different? What made him so special that the rules didn't apply to him?

"Because you have shown great integrity, loyalty and commitment to the school by sacrificing your happiness for the past seven years," Clare said. "We've all seen it. You've shut yourself away from the outside world, and the only time your face ever true lights up, is when Kitty is around. Yet for seven years, you've made no attempt to act on your feelings, you've never behaved inappropriately around her, and you've continued to put your role as headteacher first. None of us felt like you deserved to be punished when you finally got your act together and asked Kitty out for dinner."

Before Anthony could respond, the door opened. The singing stopped instantly, and a masked gunman entered the room.

Anthony knew the gunman was coming for him. He looked over at the now silent group of teenage girls.

"Close your eyes," he told them. "It's O.K., girls. It's all going to be O.K. Just close your eyes and don't open them until Miss Knight or Miss Cribb tell you to.

The girls closed their eyes and cuddled up to each other. He turned his attention to his colleagues and friends.

"They've come for me," he told them. "If I don't make it back, promise me, you'll tell Kitty."

Pain burned through him as the recoil pad of a shotgun smashed into his cheekbone. Blood filled his mouth, and he spat it out.

"Tell her," he said again. "Tell her that I love her and that even if she can't admit it, I know she loves me too."

"Ah, that's sweet Bruv," the gunman said sarcastically, as he yanked Anthony to his feet. "Maybe you're not such a cock sucker after all. Too bad the boss wants you dead anyway."

This time the recoil pad lunged hard into his abdomen, and Anthony dropped to his knees, coughing.

"Stop," he said between coughs. He got to his feet and turned to face the gunman.

"What did you say, Bruv?" the gunman asked.

"If you want to beat me, you can go right ahead," Anthony said. "But you will not beat me in front of children. Let's take it outside."

The second blow to his abdomen was worse than the first, and he fell back to his knees. He gasped for breath and coughed before spitting out more blood. He wasn't going to let this happen. He wasn't going to let this group of teenage girls witness any more violence. They'd faced enough trauma for one day. He wasn't going to add it by taking a beating in front of them.

"It's O.K., girls," he choked. "Just keep your eye closed. Remember my promise. Everything is going to be O.K."

He nodded at Clare, and she moved quickly. Anthony saw her crawl over to the girls, pulling as many of them toward her as possible, encouraging them to huddle. She began to sing. The girls started to sing. Jenny began to sing. Anthony's heart swelled with pride. These ten extraordinary young ladies and these two strong, protective women were enough to get him through the worst pain. It gave him the strength he needed to act and get himself away from the girls before they heard any more violence.

He rose to his feet again, but this time he charged at the gunman. He lunged at his legs, knocking him to the ground. They were out of the room, and Anthony laid on the ground and kicked the door shut.

"I told you I will not be beaten in front of children," he panted. "I told you to take it outside."

Before he could say anything else, though, the masked man sat up quickly, pointing the shotgun at Anthony's face.

Nineteen

Panic and dread swept through Kitty like the Great Fire of London. This couldn't be happening; it just couldn't. They had come so far; they had been so close. It couldn't be over now. *Don't do this to me now, universe. Please not now.*

"Kate," she said, hearing the panic in her own voice. "It's stopped."

"I know," Kate sighed. "I'm sorry, Kitty."

"What's happening?" Peter asked.

Kitty held out her hand. The little blood marble had stopped dancing. She began to slow down, flashing her hazard lights. She had to get everyone together. She had to do the spell again. Only this time, she would concentrate harder and make it last longer. Anthony had trusted her; he had bled for her. She couldn't let him down now. She just couldn't.

"Here?" Kate asked. "You want to do it here?"

"We don't have a choice," Kitty said as she continued to slow down. "We have less than five minutes before they turn back into a puddly mess, and there are more than enough cops to close the road."

"Kitty, we can't just stop in the middle of the A3," Peter said, referring to the name of the dual carriageway they were on.

"Bloody well watch me," Kitty said.

Nothing was going to keep her from achieving her goal of getting those kids, teachers and Anthony home. Nothing was going to stop her from getting Fitz to a hospital if it wasn't already too late. Nothing was going to stop her from taking down those bastard terrorists and saving the man she loved. Nothing.

She would get everyone out of there and home to their families if it was the last thing she ever did. She didn't care if she had to stop in the middle of the road another dozen times. She was going to keep that blood spell going.

"No," Kate yelled excitedly. "Don't stop. Keep going."

"What?" Kitty and Peter asked in unison.

"Do not stop this vehicle," Kate demanded.

"Kitty, your homing beacon has been activated. Anthony's on Hayling Island."

"Hayling Island?" Kitty asked. "Are you sure?"

"Yes," Kate said. She was practically screaming and bouncing up and down in her seat. Kitty knew she had to be sure to be this excited.

In that brief moment, Kitty had to fight the urge to cry. She knew where Anthony was. She knew how to get to him, and she knew it wouldn't take long to get there. She was going to find him, and she was going to rescue him. The universe had given her exactly what she needed after all; thank the goddess. Now all she needed was to be sure that the hostages were with him so that she and her team could get them home safely too.

"Keep an eye on that tracker Kate," Kitty demanded. "I want to know if there is the slightest movement."

"You've got it, Kit," Kate said. "I've also saved the current data on the tracker. That way, if the beacon goes offline for any reason, we'll still know exactly where we're going."

Kitty sped up again and turned off the SUV's hazard lights. It took only seconds for her to get back up to ninety.

Hold on, Anthony, she pleaded silently. *Just hold on*.

They would be on Hayling Island in less than twenty minutes. Kitty knew as she had done this drive many times. Granted, she usually drove much slower than this, and she usually had the twins, buckets and spades, towels and a cool box in the car, but at least she was confident she knew exactly where she was going and how long it would take her to get there at ninety miles an hour.

She listened as Kate radioed into the other vehicles. Her excitement was evident in her tone. "All units, please be advised, we believe the hostages are on Hayling Island. We have a positive trace on the homing beacon. I repeat the hostages may be on Hayling Island."

Kitty felt no such excitement, though. She felt nothing but nervous anticipation. She wanted to know exactly what they were walking into. She wanted to know what state Fitz was in and how the other hostages were holding up, and she wanted to know whether or not she would get there on time to stop Anthony from being executed.

Dread filled the pit of her stomach. What if she was too late? What if she got there and Anthony was dead? How would she live with losing someone else she loved? No, he had to survive. Surely the universe wouldn't give him to her and then snatch him away so cruelly. Surely that couldn't happen to her twice.

She couldn't be sure. The only thing she was sure of, was when she got there, if Anthony was alive, Kitty would tell him she loved him, and she would keep telling him every day for the rest of her life.

Anthony stared down the barrel of the shotgun pointed at his face. He knew if he was sensible, he would be scared, but burning anger was all he felt.

"What are you waiting for?" he demanded. "Do you want to put it on bloody YouTube? Shoot me, you fucking son of a bitch."

He was sitting on an old wooden chair in a dark, damp, foul-smelling room. His hands were bound on his lap, and his legs were tied to the two front legs of the rickety chair.

"Now, why would I shoot you, Bruv?" the gunman asked. "My men heard you in there. You're well tight with the feds, and you're gonna tell me everything."

Finally, Anthony was face to face with the man from the YouTube video. He knew it because he had memorised that voice. There was no doubt about it. This was the racist son of a bitch responsible for Fitz's injuries. This was the man who had ordered Anthony's failed execution attempt and had publicly announced he wanted to kill him.

"If I know so much, how come I don't you know your name?" Anthony asked. "In polite society, you at least know the name of someone who is holding the gun to your head."

"But this ain't no polite society Bruv," the man said. "But you can call me Guv."

"Well then, Guv," Anthony said. "Tell me why you're doing this. Why are you holding children hostage?"

"This country is fucked up, mate," Guv said. There's ya royals, ya corrupt government, darkies walking the streets like they own the place, women dressing like whores when they should be in the home. Cock sucking arse bandits wandering around freely, flying their fucking great rainbow flags like shoving dicks up their arses is something to be proud of. God didn't plan none of this, Bruv."

"God?" Anthony asked. "Don't make me laugh."

"You think this is funny?" Guv asked.

"I find nothing funny in you using God as an excuse to commit acts of terrorism against this country. I find nothing funny in you holding children hostage in some attempt to win a pissing contest because you don't like our country's views on race and gender equality."

"Don't forget the homos," Guv said. "God hates the queers."

Anthony's blood boiled. He wasn't a religious man. He believed in science. He believed in evolution, and that dinosaurs walked the earth. He didn't believe in God or some big universal life force watching over everyone. He firmly believed in equal rights, though. He ran a school that was open to everyone, no matter their race, gender or sexual orientation. He was proud to lead an all-inclusive community.

He had friends of all different races, sexual preferences and gender identities, and he loved them all. What these bastards had done to Fitz was unforgivable. Fitz was like a brother to him, and these bastards had nearly beaten him to death because his skin was black. It made him sick to even think about it.

"You're from London," Anthony said. "Were you born here?"

"I was born in this fucking shithole country, yeah Bruv," Guv answered. "What of it?"

"This shithole country that welcomes people of all faiths and cultures," Anthony said, rolling his eyes. "In committing acts of terrorism against this country, you are committing acts of terrorism against the countless straight white men and innocent children who live here."

"We are freeing them," Guv said. "When me and my brothers come to power, this shit show of a country will be free for all straight white men. We'll be equal."

"If you opened your eyes," Anthony said sarcastically, "You would see that your plan for domination is actually based on anything but equality. This country isn't holding straight white men hostage. They are free to get an education, work, practice any faith, be part of communities and worship according to their own beliefs. In this country we are free to work as teachers, work in retail, in the NHS, in government, own land, drive cars, and go to university."

"Stop," Guv demanded. "I will not hear of what straight white men can do in this country. You have no business speaking of being straight. You're a tainted arse bandit."

"Actually, I'm straight, and you're an uneducated idiot," Anthony shot. "You're completely fucked in the head."

Guv slapped Anthony hard across the face. He felt the chair crack slightly as he was jolted and realised all he had to do was push this lunatic a little harder. If he could get the chair to break, he'd be able to get free. Then he would show Guv that he knew precisely how to overpower him, even with a gun pointed at him.

"You hit like a pussy," Anthony mocked. "If you want to fight, untie me, and I'll teach you to fight like a real man After all, you want to be a real man, don't you Guv?"

"I swear, I ain't playing games with you, Bruv," Guv growled. "Now tell me about them feds."

"I am not your Bruv," Anthony snapped. "My brother is the black guy that you bastards beat to a pulp today, and you're nothing but a twisted little maggot with a big gun."

"The feds," Guv warned. "Tell me."

"I know everything there is to know about that," Anthony lied. "I've been to their base of operations. I know the names of everyone involved in every operation to take down your band of thugs. They gave me the grand tour when they tried to recruit me."

"You will tell me," Guv insisted.

"I ain't telling you shit until you release the hostages Bruv," Anthony mocked. "Let them go, and I'll tell you what you need to know."

"Tell me now," Guv yelled. "Or I'll go in there and start beating on that crop."

"Women," Anthony corrected. "They are girls and women. They aren't your crop; they're human beings."

Guv looked furious and Anthony laughed.

Come on, you son of a bitch, come and get me, Anthony willed.

He didn't like violence. He hadn't studied boxing and mixed martial arts because he enjoyed violence. He had studied them because he was athletic and enjoyed contact sports. He also enjoyed giving the punching bag in the gym a good beating every now than then. Yet, he'd never once been violent to another human being. Given a chance, though, he would fight his way out of this building, taking down every one of these crazy bastards if it meant getting his friends and students out of here, and getting Fitz to a hospital.

Guv lowered his rifle and leant in close to Anthony, his face burning with rage. He opened his mouth to speak but never got the chance as Anthony took his shot.

He rocked back in the chair and then lunged forward, bringing his head crashing down on Guv's nose with an almighty crack.

Guv dropped the gun, wobbled and fell to the floor clutching his very bloody, very broken nose. Anthony leant as far forward in the chair as he could and then threw himself back as hard as he could, keeping his chin to his chest so as not to smash his head on the ground. The old wooden chair splintered and broke to pieces, freeing Anthony's legs.

He scrambled to his feet.

Guv tried to get to his first, but Anthony was too fast.

He leapt into the air, lifted his leg and spun all at once, delivering a clean roundhouse to the side of Guv's head, knocking him flat out.

"That's for Fitz, you son of a bitch," Anthony growled as he landed smoothly and rushed to pick up the rifle.

"What the fuck am I supposed to do with this?" he muttered.

He hated guns more than he hated any other kind of violence. Yes, he enjoyed contact sports, boxing, kickboxing and mixed martial arts, but there was respect, discipline and control in the way those events unfolded. Guns were the weapons of madmen. You didn't need any form of discipline or self-control to use a gun. Any idiot could shoot somebody.

Anthony had never before used what he could do in a real-life scenario. He had never needed to defend himself in real life, and even though there were thirteen lives at risk in another part of the warehouse, he did not feel partially proud of himself in that moment.

Still, he had no time to think about it. He had no time to think about the pain ripping through his body or the fact that that once again, his earlier gunshot wound was bleeding.

He crouched down beside Guv and set the rifle down. His hands still bound, Anthony began to search Guv's unconscious body. He had to have a knife.

"Yes," he gasped as he pulled a flick knife from Guv's pocket.

Anthony sat, pulled his feet together, bringing them toward his body. He kept his pelvis wide and his knees out to the side. Carefully he opened the flick knife and nestled it between the outer soles of his trainers, pressing his feet firmly together. Separating his hands as much as he could, he carefully fed them over the knife and began to rub the cable tie up and down against the blade.

The cable tie broke apart, and Anthony grabbed the knife, closed it and shoved it into the pocket of tracksuit bottoms. He scrambled to his knees and continued to search Guv. He found a mobile phone and more cable ties. He used Guv's thumbprint to unlock the phone before setting it down on the floor and then tied his would-be assassin's hands together. Unlike Guv had done, Anthony took the time to bind his hands behind his back, knowing it would make it damn near impossible for him to use the gun if he regained consciousness.

Anthony picked up the phone from the floor. He had made a point of memorising Kitty's mobile phone number before he left school, and now he was thankful that he had. He typed the number into the phone and pressed the call button.

Twenty

Kitty could feel the knots in her stomach getting tighter as she drove over the bridge that would take them onto Hayling Island. They were close, but what would she find when she got there? She was sure Jenny, Claire and the students would all be unharmed, but what of Fitz and Anthony? What state would they be in?

She had spent much of the last ten minutes torturing herself. She cared about getting everyone home safely. Getting all of the hostages out alive was her top priority. Yet, all she had really been able to focus on was finding Anthony. She'd never had a personal entanglement complicate an assignment before. She was struggling to separate her feelings for Anthony from her mission. She felt cruel and selfish. She didn't want her potential boyfriend to prioritise Fitz, Jenny, Clare, or the kids, but he did in her heart. In her heart, she wanted to find him above anyone else, and she was ashamed of herself for that.

Anthony's life wasn't more precious to her than the other hostages' lives were to their loved ones. She should be able to find a balance. She had never separated one hostage over another before. Why was she starting to do that now? She tried to think about it rationally. Anyone of those girls' parents would prioritise their child over any other hostage. Clare's husband would prioritise his wife over Jenny. Yet, she wasn't just a woman looking for the man she loved. She was a professional, and rescuing hostages was her job.

Anthony had risked his life so she could get all of the hostages out safely, and she knew the kids needed to be her top priority. Whatever happened, making sure they were safe had to be her first objective.

She slowed down, turned off the flashing lights lighting up her car like a beacon, and looked in her rear-view mirror. The vehicles behind her echoed her and turned their lights off too. She didn't want to arrive on Hayling Island lit up like a Christmas tree. She didn't want to announce her arrival too soon. She also didn't want to disturb those on the island who lived there and would be sleeping.

The music on S.U.V.'s entertainment system cut out as her phone began to ring through the speakers.

She tapped the call answer button on her steering wheel.

"Yeah," she said in the way of an answer.

"Kitty?"

"Anthony," she gasped. Her heart slammed in her chest, and she had to fight the sudden urge to burst into tears. "Oh my god, Anthony, are you alright?"

Hearing Anthony's voice was like a dream come true for her. She had never known relief quite like it. Her heart started to race, and her hands began to tremble. *He's alive. Anthony's alive.*

"A little battered but still ruggedly handsome," he replied.

A round of cheers and whoops ricocheted through the car.

"Where are you?" Kitty asked, "What happened? How are you calling me?"

"I memorised your number before I left," Anthony said. "Then when Guv here let his guard down, I broke his nose and walloped him in the side of the head with a roundhouse. He's now taking a little nap."

"You are so hot," Kate said.

"Kate," Kitty snapped.

"Sorry," Kate said.

Anthony laughed.

"Tell me the homing beacon worked," Anthony said. "Tell me you're nearly here, Kitty."

Kitty knew Anthony wasn't feeling quite as brave and heroic as he was pretending to be. He sounded exhausted, in pain and frightened.

"Oh, it worked, you clever, clever man," She told him. "We've just crossed over onto Hayling Island. We're just minutes away from you now."

"I'm on Hayling Island?" Anthony asked.

"Yes," Kitty said.

"There's a smashing fish and chip shop here," Anthony mused.

"Well, when this is all over, you can buy me dinner," Kitty said.

When all of this was over, she was never letting Anthony out of her sight again. When all of this was over, she would tell him she loved him and beg him to move away with her. Kitty wanted a life away from all of this. She wanted a life with just Anthony and her girls.

"It is almost over, isn't it, Kitty?" he asked.

"Very soon, babe," she promised.

He sounded so tired. He had to be exhausted, emotional and in agony.

"How are the hostages?" Walters called from the back seat.

"Fitz is in a bad state," Anthony said, sounding tense suddenly. "Last I saw him, he wasn't conscious. He's been badly beaten, had some broken bones and probably some internal bleeding. Everyone else is smelly, dirty and traumatised, but otherwise, fine. Jenny might need that gash on her head looking at though, once she knows Fitz is being looked after."

"How long have you been away from them?" Kitty asked.

"About half an hour," he said. "I'm stuck in a room with Sleeping Beauty here and waiting for him to wake up so that he and I can take a little walk."

"No," Kitty said quickly. "Just holdfast. We're going to be there in just a few minutes." We're abandoning our vehicles and coming in silently on foot."

"Hostages first," Anthony said. "I'm fine here. Just get everyone else out first."

"I promise," Kitty said, even though he hadn't actually asked her to promise. "I need to go now, Anthony, but I promise we'll be there soon."

"Hurry," Anthony said. "I'm not sure how much longer Fitz can hand on."

"In half an hour, he'll be in a chopper and on his way to a hospital, Ant, I promise. Just sit tight and don't do anything reckless."

"You know me," Anthony said.

"And that's the problem," Kitty told him. "I'll see you soon."

As Kitty disconnected the call, she had to fight the urge to cry. *He's alive. Anthony's alive. The hostages are alive. You're going to get everyone home.* She repeated the words in her head, over and over.

"You O.K?" Peter asked.

Kitty sniffed and nodded. "Honesty, I thought the stupid son of a bitch would have gotten himself killed by now."

"You don't give him enough credit," Peter told her. "He's much more capable than you realise."

"I know that," Kitty sighed. "But so was Jack. He was the most capable man I ever met."

"And what happened to him happened because he was in a war zone," Peter reminded her.

"I know," Kitty sniffed as she fought back the tears that threatened to spill over. "I just want this over. I just want him safe. I want all of them to be safe."

"They will be," Peter assured her. "In no time at all, you'll be getting those kids home to their parents, and you'll have Fitz airborne. This is what you do, Kitty, and you're brilliant at it. Don't forget that."

"Thanks, Pete," Kitty whispered as a single tear finally slipped down her cheek.

They drove a little further before Kitty pulled over and switched off the engine on a quiet dirt track. She unclipped her seatbelt and took a steadying breath.

She was ready.

"Let's go save some kids," she said as she opened her door.

She got out of the S.U.V. and headed to the tailgate at the back as everyone else got out and followed her. She took out her helmet and put it on her head, securing it in place. Her long hair was tied in a tight plait running down her back and hanging over the top of her tactical vest.

It was go time.

Kitty rounded up her coven and began issuing their orders, assigning each of them a team to work with. She also assigned one person to remain with each vehicle with the instructions to stay on standby until someone activated a homing beacon.

Finally, she turned to her team.

"Our objective is to rescue the hostages," she said. "Students and staff first, and then Anthony."

"Got it," Peter said.

Kitty continued.

"Thorpe, you'll help Walters carry the medical equipment, Peter, you'll cover them. Kate, you and I are going in hot and heavy with the spell work."

"Kitty," Kate began.

"You've got this, Kate," Kitty said gently as she patted Kate's arm. "It's time you got back in the field."

Kate nodded but didn't say a word, and Kitty could feel her unease.

Operation Castledown had left a huge emotional wound for Kate that refused to heal. Her energy levels had been too high that day. She hadn't been focused, and the explosion she had created killed two people. It had been a tragic accident, but Kate hadn't been able to forgive herself, and she hadn't been back in the field since.

"It's going to be just fine, Kate," she assured her. "You know you can do this."

Kitty didn't wait for Kate to respond this time. She knew that if she did, it would give Kate longer to hesitate and doubt herself. She started walking and left Kate and the others to follow. This kind of mission meant there would be no circle casting, no grounding and no taking their time to prepare. This kind of mission meant responding to any situation as quickly as possible with the magic they could muster in the moment. That wasn't to say they were going to wing it and hope for the best. Kitty and her team had spent years training and practising their craft. They knew how to channel their magic quickly and effectively.

Kate had been training every day for months. Kitty was certain she could now use her explosive powers safely without grounding as long as she had an anchor. Kitty was going to be Kate's anchor.

They walked in silence, Kitty leading the way with Kate by her side. Kate had already pulled up an aerial view of the warehouse and the grounds surrounding it in the S.U.V, and had forwarded it on to everyone on the task force before they had crossed onto Hayling Island. Everyone knew exactly what their point of entry was. Kitty knew with a member of her coven leading each tactical team that everyone would be in the right places at the right time.

The closer they got to the warehouse, the slower they moved. They grouched down low and moved purposefully. Kitty drew her firearm, knowing she would use it only as a last resort. Kate and Peter followed suit. Walters and Thorpe focused on carrying medical equipment but were armed should the team take fire.

They could see the ground surrounding the back of the warehouse now, and Kitty held up a hand to signal that they should stop. They were close enough that they could now use their first spell. Kitty and Kate had created this one together some years ago. It was a firm favourite of Kitty's as it allowed them to see through walls in a way that thermal imaging could not.

Kitty signalled to Walters and Thorpe to set down their medical bags and take out their weapons. They would need to cover Kitty and Kate for the next few minutes as they handled the magic.

She pulled out two pairs of sunglasses from the cargo pocket at her left thigh and laid them on the ground. She nodded to Kate, who presented her with a small corked bottle. The bottle contained a mixture of gold, green and purple glitter. To anyone else, it would look simply like the stuff of crafts. Still, in reality, it had taken months of careful planning and a lot of trial and error to get the spell just right.

Each colour of glitter had been carefully enchanted to allow a pair of sunglasses to see heat signatures through buildings, each colour representing different people. Gold highlighted innocents, green highlighted targets and purple highlighted tactical.

Kitty re-holstered her sidearm, took the glitter from Kate, uncorked the bottle and sprinkled some of the glitter into her hand. She passed her bottle back to Kate and put her hands together. She rubbed them over the glasses and recited her spell.

"See inside this building we must, with the magic of this glitter we trust. Help us set these innocents free and return them to their families."

As the glitter hit the glasses and her words were said, a small burst of energy shot through Kitty, telling her the spell was complete and the glasses were ready for use.

Kitty knew that the other members of her coven would be performing the same spell at that exact moment. She also knew that no matter how much they had tried, they could not get the glasses to work for those who were not magically inclined, meaning they couldn't just hand out pairs to all members of the task force. It was something Kitty and Kate were still working on and trying to figure out.

She picked up the glasses, passed a pair to Kate, and they both put them on. Kitty blinked a few times and then looked straight at the building ahead of her. In the room directly ahead, Kitty could see thirteen figures. Eleven were huddled together in a group. One was sat further away, cradling what was obviously an unconscious Fitz. They were all gold and sparkly and but were still clearly recognisable as human forms.

Beyond that, Kitty could make out a door. On the other side of the door, the green sparkly form of one of the terrorists could be seen.

Kitty had to stop herself from looking beyond what was right in front of her. She wanted to look further and look for Anthony, but she knew she needed to focus on the task at hand and not get distracted.

She turned her attention to Kate.

"You ready?" she asked.

"Not remotely," Kate said.

"Take my hand," Kitty said. "Let me anchor you. If it feels like too much power, just let it flow into me, just like we practised."

Kate nodded and took Kitty's outstretched hand. Kitty reached for her radio and clicked down the little button that allowed her to speak.

"All units, go, go, go!" She called as she and Kate got to their feet.

Each holding the hands between them, they marched forward quickly. They sidestepped to the right until they were sure they were sufficiently far enough away from the hostages in the building ahead of them. Kitty gave Kate's hand a gentle squeeze.

It was all she needed to do for both women to throw their hands out in front of them.

Kate shot explosive energy through her body and out through her hand. Kitty pulled the energy back into her own body, drawing the force back toward herself.

The result was an almighty explosion that ripped down half the wall with Kate's energy. Kitty used her energy to pull the debris from the fallen wall back out and onto the ground outside, ensuring no one inside was harmed by the force of the explosion.

Screams erupted from inside the room, and the door at the far end of the room burst open.

"Down," Peter yelled.

Kitty and Kate dropped to the floor just in time for Peter to take out the entering gunman with his sidearm. A single headshot killed the terrorist instantly and he fell to the floor.

More screams echoed into the night, along with the sound of gunshots from outside the warehouse. Kitty scrambled back to her feet and ran forward into the room, her team hot on her heels.

"You did it, Kate," she yelled as she ran. "You clever, clever girl."

There was no hint of debris inside the building, and no one had been close enough to the explosion to get hurt. Kate had found her power, and Kitty was immensely proud of her.

Kitty stopped, pulled off the sunglasses and sunk to her knees in front of the terrified teenagers.

"Shh," she soothed. "It's O.K. You're safe now. Shh, you're alright. It's all over, girls. You're going home."

The girls began to cry, and Kitty recognised the sounds. They were the unmasked sounds hostages made when they realised they were finally safe. The girls held nothing back as they clung to each other and wept openly. They knew they were going home, and they were relieved beyond measure.

Kitty turned quickly to her team. Kate was already standing guard at the door with her gun drawn as Peter did the same from the hole Kitty and Kate had made in the wall. Walters and Thorpe had already carefully extracted Fitz from Jenny's arms, and Thorpe was assisting Walters in examining him.

She turned to Jenny and Clare.

"Are you two alright?" she asked softly.

Both women burst into tears in unison. Kitty scrambled forward, pulling them both into her arms.

"You survived," she said to them as she hugged them tightly. "You're safe, and you're going home. Your families are waiting at school for you."

She turned to the group of teenage girls while still hugging Jenny and Clare.

"That goes for you beautiful, brave, darling girls as well," she told them. "Your families are all waiting for you and are desperate to see you. We're going to get a team of doctors and nurses to look at you, and then we are getting you all back to your parents."

She turned to Clare. "And there's a little girl at school who is desperate to see her mummy."

Clare nodded as the tears fell freely.

"Thank you, Kitty; thank you so much," she choked.

Suddenly Jenny sat bolt upright, almost knocking Kitty on her arse.

"Anthony," she said quickly. "They took him. He said to tell you if he didn't come back that he loves you."

Kitty nodded, released Clare and stood up.

"Wait here," she instructed as she turned to the group of teenagers. "Girls, I'll be right back with your headteacher."

She un-holstered her gun, cocked it and turned to Kate.

"Hit your homing beacon and get choppers and medics here now," Kitty told Kate. "I'm going to get my man."

Twenty-One

Kitty slipped the sunglasses back on and looked around as more members of her tactical team began to fill the room through the hole in the wall.

"Perimeter secure, General," Si said as he entered the room. "All hostiles down."

Kitty nodded her understanding, stepped over the dead terrorist and ran out of the room. She could see precisely where Anthony was through the enchanted glasses, and no surprise, he was pacing. She could also see the slumped form of the terrorist he had taken out. That must have been one hell of a roundhouse, Kitty mused as she ran. Then she looked at Anthony's sparkly form again and stopped. He might have been pacing, but he was limping quite badly. He was clearly in pain.

She set off again and ran into the main warehouse space, to small a room on the right. She was finally going to find Anthony. Her heart pounded in her chest as she ran, and she could hear her pulse in her ears. It was time to get her man and get him home. She was going to tell him she loved him, and she was going to beg him to move away with her so that they could start a safe, peaceful life together with the twins.

"Ant," she yelled as she ran. "Ant, I'm here."
She stopped as she reached the room Anthony
was in, opened the door and gasped.
In the middle of the room, stood a very bloody,
very bruised and very handsome Anthony
Richmond. She took a moment to secure her
weapon and slid it back into its holster before
running right into his open arms.
"I love you," she choked through the tears she
had finally allowed to fall. "I love you so much it
hurts. I'm so sorry I never told you earlier I was
just too scared to admit it to myself. I was scared
that if I let myself love you, I would lose you. But
I do love you, and I never want to let you go."
She felt Anthony's arms tighten around her.
"I love you too, baby," he whispered. "I'm not
going anywhere. You're stuck with me, General
Kline, whether you like it or not."
"I love it," Kitty sobbed. "And I love you."
For a few moments, Kitty stood there sobbing as
Anthony rocked her in his arms. When she finally
pulled away from him, she could see that his face
was also wet with tears.
"We have a lot to talk about," she said as she
stepped back slightly. "But first, let's get you
back to your staff and students. They're waiting
for you."

"What do we do about him?" Anthony asked of Guv. The terrorist was regaining consciousness and was slumped in the corner of the room, his hands and feet bound, one of his own socks shoved in his mouth.

Kitty turned around and looked back out into the main warehouse that was now filling up with military and police.

"Oi, you lot," she called to the crowd. "Teach has got a present for you."

"Oh, don't you bloody start calling me Teach as well," Anthony groaned as Kitty took him by the hand and led him from the room.

"Ant, then?" She asked.

"Ant is fine," he answered. "But only coming from you."

"You've got it, Ant," she laughed.

As they began to walk, Kitty could see how much Anthony was struggling. He was clearly in a lot of pain. Pain she had quickly forgotten about upon seeing him. She wondered much it had hurt him when she ran into his arms. He hadn't even flinched. Had he been trying to be brave for her benefit? He didn't need to be brave for her. Didn't he realise that?

"Do you need a wheelchair or a stretcher, babe?" she asked as she carefully wrapped an arm around him.

"No, I bloody don't," Anthony growled.

"You don't need to be brave for me," she assured him. "Ask my team how many times I've been wheeled out of missions like this instead of walking."

"I'm not being brave for you," Anthony told her. "I'm being brave for my students, who have been to hell and back today."

"Fair enough," Kitty said. "Then put your weight on me until we get close to the door. Then you can walk in on your own."

"That works," Anthony agreed.

Kitty felt him slump slightly against her.

"Better?" she asked.

"Much," he said. "Thank you."

It felt so good to Kitty to have Anthony's staggering body against hers. She had allowed herself to imagine the worst, and she had convinced herself he'd be leaving in a body bag. It almost seemed unreal that it was finally over and he was safe.

"How's Fitz?" Anthony asked as they walked. Kitty stopped walking and turned to face Anthony.

"The doctor is doing everything he can," she said softly. "Honestly though, Anthony, he doesn't look good."

She was trying so hard to be strong for Anthony, but she couldn't help the tears that spilled over and ran down her cheeks.

Anthony wiped the tears from her face, and she leaned into him slightly, trying not to cause him any more pain.

"Fitz will be alright," Anthony said. "He's as tough as old boots. You'll see."

They began walking again. As they got to the room where the hostages were waiting to be evacuated, Kitty was glad to see that the body of the gunman Peter had taken down had been dragged out. She didn't want the girls to have to keep looking at a dead body. Kitty wasn't sure how long it would take them to come to terms with what had happened to them or the fact that they had witnessed someone being shot in the head, but she didn't want to have the reminder in full view of them. She knew that Peter had had no choice when he made the call and took the shot. He hadn't hesitated at all. It had been a good shot, and it had saved lives.

"What the hell happened to the wall?" Anthony asked as they approached the room.

"That would be Kate's explosive personality," Kitty grinned. She was so proud of Kate for letting go of her fear and blasting that hole. It had taken a lot for her to be able to do that after what happened during Castledown.

"Remind me never to piss her off," Anthony said, interrupting her thoughts.

Kitty laughed and released Anthony, as she had promised. She paused, squeezed his hand, and walked ahead of him into the room.

Before she knew what was happening, Anthony was swarmed by teenage girls who pulled him into a group hug.

"Girls, I really shouldn't," he protested.

"Just go with it," Clare said as she and Jenny joined in the hug. "Just this once."

"I don't think the rules on hugging apply tonight," Kitty said. "Certainly, as an S.H.P. parent, I have no concerns or objections."

"Besides," Jenny chimed in. "We're surrounded by police officers. They can arrest us after if they really want."

"There'll be no arresting of teachers tonight," Peter said as he moved to stand next to Kitty. "Hugs all around."

Kitty pulled Peter to her and hugged him fiercely. "Thank you," she whispered.

"You're welcome," he whispered back.

"Everyone out now," Walters yelled suddenly, and Kitty pulled back from Peter quickly. The hugs and chatter stopped, and the room fell silent instantly.

Oh goddess. Kitty knew a command like that meant only one thing.

She didn't have to say anything. Her team stepped forward, easing everyone quickly and quietly from the room.

"It's alright, girls," Clare said. "Let's go."

Jenny didn't move. Anthony didn't move. Kitty moved back over to Anthony and took his hand.

Jenny shrugged off the police officer trying to lead her from the room.

"I'm not leaving," Jenny said firmly.

"Kitty," Anthony whispered.

"I understand," she said, squeezing his hand before saying firmly, "She stays."

Kitty released Anthony's hand, and together they stepped forward, and each placed an arm around Jenny's back.

"Thank you," Jenny whispered as tears rolled down her cheeks.

They all stood in horrified silence as Walters and Thorpe worked tirelessly, giving Fitz C.P.R.

Come on, Fitz, Kitty willed silently. *Not now, please not now. We've come too far. You've held on for so long. Don't give up now. Don't you dare give up.*

"We need to get him to a trauma centre if he's going to have a chance," Walters called over his shoulder, panting from the physical exhaustion of giving Fitz C.P.R.

"There's an Army base in Portsmouth with a trauma centre," Kitty said as she released her hold on Jenny and crouched down next to Walters. "Choppers are landing now."

She turned to Jenny and put out her hand. Jenny stepped forward and took it.

"Take his hand," Kitty said. "Don't let him be alone. Talk to him. Let him know you are close."

Jenny nodded and did as Kitty said. She knelt, took Fitz's hand and began to talk to him about all the plans they had made together for the future. How they were going to divide her wardrobe, who was going to clean the toilet, who was going to cook each night. She talked to him about all the things that came from living together.

Kitty stood up and stepped back, allowing them some privacy. She took Anthony's hand and gently pulled him to one side.

"Can't you do anything?" he asked.

"I really wish I could," Kitty said. "If his wounds were mystical, I could try, but not with mortal wounds caused by another human being. I'm so sorry."

A medical team rushed into the room and stepped in to help Walters with his efforts to save Fitz. Kitty turned to Thorpe, who had stepped back to let the medics take over.

"Come on," she said, taking him by the elbow. "Let's get you some air."

She led Thorpe from the room, and Anthony followed. As she stepped outside, she saw that various medical teams had arrived. There were ambulances with paramedics, Army doctors and nurses on site. Each of the students and Clare were being checked over as well as two members of Kitty's task force who had received minor injuries during the takedown.

Kitty waved a doctor over to where she was standing.

"See that Teach gets looked after," she said.

"Kitty," Anthony began, but she cut him off.

"Hard restraints and a sedative should do it if he resists."

She gave Anthony a gentle nudge on his way and turned to Thorpe.

"You did really well tonight, Thorpe," she said. "I'm proud of you."

"Thank you, General," he said politely, but she could tell he was shaken up and doubting what she said.

He was covered in Fitz's blood and trembling slightly. Kitty knew precisely what he was going through as she had been through it several times. The first time in Iraq was when she was around Thorpe's age.

"This isn't going to mean much to you now, Thorpe," she said. "But I am promoting you to the rank of Corporal and putting you forward for a commendation. You are a fine asset to the team Thorpe, and I am honoured to serve with you."

Thorpe nodded but said nothing, so she led him over to the back of an ambulance, removed his tactical vest and sat him down on the steps. Corporal Thorpe has been a true hero tonight," she told the student paramedic who was gathering supplies in the ambulance. "He's served his country with bravery and honour. Let's see that he gets a blanket and something warm and sweet to drink."

That was code for I have a patient suffering from shock. Kitty knew the student understood the reference as she nodded.

"Yes, Ma'am," the student said as she grabbed a blanket and hopped down from the back of the ambulance, taking Thorpe's hand in hers.

"I'm Nikki, she said. "And who might you be?"

"Thorpe," he said quietly.

"Got a first name Thorpe?" she asked.

"Danny," he said.

"Well, Danny," she said. "Do you think you could please tell me if any of this blood is yours?"

Thorpe shook his head but didn't say anything, so Kitty intervened.

"It's not his," she said. "He's been working hard to save a life."

"You should join the ambulance service," Nikki told Thorpe.

"No can do," Kitty said. "There's no way I'm letting go of this one without a fight."

Kitty heard running footsteps and loud chatter behind her and turned to see Fitz being carried on a stretcher to the waiting helicopter. In the middle of the hustle, Jenny just stood there, not knowing what to do as Fitz was loaded on the chopper, so Kitty ran over to her.

"Come on," she said, taking her hand and pulling her gently. "Stay low."

Kitty led Jenny to the chopper, opened the front door, leant in and grabbed a headset.

"She's coming with you, Rocket Man," Kitty called into the mic and pointing at Jenny. "See to it that she is treated like royalty when you get to the base. She works for Teach, and that's her man they're loading into the back. And make sure someone takes a look at her. She had a fall earlier and is a bit bashed up."

"I'll take good care of her, Boss," Rocket Man called loudly into the headset as he patted the seat next to him.

Kitty dumped the head set back in the chopper and turned to Jenny.

"Get in," Kitty yelled to her over the noise of the blades.

She helped Jenny get into the chopper and get secure. The chopper doors all closed, and Kitty stepped back, allowing it to take off.

"Don't you dare die, Fitz," she said quietly as she watched the chopper take off into the night sky. One by one, Clare and the students were cleared to leave and were loaded into two choppers. When they were all finally on board, Kate and Peter each got into one of the two choppers. Finally, Kitty watched as they headed back to school. Kitty was so relieved knowing that there would be some very happy reunions taking place in no time at all.

She took a moment and stopped to text her daughters in their group chat thread.

All is well here. Your friends are safe in helicopters on their way back to school. I have to stay here for a while longer, but I promise I am O.K. It's all over now.
Get some sleep, and I'll see you both in the morning. Love you to the moon and back.
Mum xx

Now that she'd let her daughters know she was safe and all was well, Kitty turned her focus back to Anthony, who she could hear kicking up a fuss.

"I'm not going to the hospital," he insisted. "I'm fine. I really don't need to go."

"Anthony Richmond," she said hotly as she marched over to where he sat on a stretcher. "I swear if you don't get to the hospital this minute, I'll tie you down and take you right now."

Kitty regretted the words as soon as they were out of her mouth. She felt eyes burning into her from all directions. Cheers and whoops echoed across the darkness.

"Oh, fuck off and do some work, you lot," she shouted, but even she couldn't help but laugh at herself.

"Seriously, babe," she said quietly. "I'm no doctor, but that arm needs cleaning and stitching again, your cheekbone might be fractured, and you need a C.T. scan to check for internal bleeding."

"Exactly what I just told him," the doctor said, treating Anthony said. "Let's hope he listens to you better than he listens to me."

"I don't have time to spend hours in a hospital waiting room," Anthony said. "I need to get back to school. I need to get back to see Fitz's family.

"You're not going to mainstream hospital, Ant," Kitty told him.

Anthony and the doctor both looked equally surprised.

"You are still a key part of an ongoing MI5-MoD operation," she said. "Until such a time that changes, you are under military protection. So let's get you in a chopper, get you to our nearest trauma centre and get you looked at. I'll call ahead and make sure you get an x-ray and a C.T. as soon as you land. If there's nothing of concern, they'll have you patched up and back in the air within an hour. And it'll allow you to check on Jenny and Fitz."

"Fine," Anthony sighed. "You're right. I know you're right."

"I usually am," Kitty smirked.

"You coming for the ride?" Anthony asked.

"Oh, believe me, I would love to," Kitty said. "Unfortunately, though, I still have a couple of hours of work to do here before I can leave. I'll see you back at school later, though."

She leant in and kissed him gently.

"I love you," he breathed against her lips.

"I love you too," She whispered.

With that, Anthony finally laid down on the stretcher and closed his eyes. Kitty hated watching him leave as he was loaded into the helicopter, but she still had work to do on-site. There was a body recovery and clean-up mission to oversee, people to debrief, and a lot of paperwork waiting for her.

She turned to her team and called, "Right, you lot. Let's get to work."

Twenty-Two

Anthony rolled over carefully, trying not to catch the cannula in his hand on anything as he reached for his phone from his bedside table. He checked the time. It was just after eight o'clock. He'd only been dozing on and off for a few minutes at a time since he got into bed just after six o'clock. Thanks to the morphine he'd been given, he was in considerably less pain, and he was completely wiped out. Yet, he felt too sick, fidgety and unsettled to sleep.

Anthony had refused the morphine until he was tucked up in his own bed. He needed to see for himself that Clare, his students and their families were safe and settled. He needed to see Fitz's family before they were taken to the Army hospital in Portsmouth. He needed to check in with the staff and students who had remained on-site.

He was the headteacher, and the entire school community had just been through a traumatic experience. Therefore, he had point-blank refused to have any drugs before he had done everything he had to do and spoken to everyone he had to talk to.

He'd seen Clare fast asleep on a crash mat in the sports hall with Bo and Chris. He chatted briefly to Clare's parents, who were going to head over to her house and pick her up some fresh clothes as she had refused to leave school until there was news on Jenny and Fitz.

He'd prepared a statement from his laptop that he'd emailed over to Kate, had approved, and posted on the school website and social media accounts. It didn't go into too much detail stating only that staff and students on the way home from the netball final had become the victims of a terrorist attack. They had been rescued by a special task force, and that everyone was safe and well, aside from Fitz, whose condition he was unable to comment on at this early stage.

He gave no specific information about the task force, the rescue operation or details of Fitz's injuries. He also opted not to include any information about how he had come to receive his own injuries. He simply said that he was under medical orders to take some time off to heal and would be handing the reins over to the two school deputy headteachers for the time being.

He'd also said that all students and Clare were physically unharmed. They would be going home with their families and taking an extended break from school to allow them to begin to process the psychological effects of what they had been through. Finally, he had said that Jenny was being treated in hospital for minor injuries, which was partially true. She had been treated and was being monitored. She was mostly there as she didn't want to leave Fitz, though. Anthony had chosen to leave that information out of his statement, allowing Jenny and Fitz's relationship to remain private.

At six o'clock, he had closed his laptop and finally accepted the morphine as well as a bag of IV fluids. He'd declined fluids at the hospital as he has been keen to return to school. He hitched a ride back in the chopper with a small team of medics who were going to remain on-site for the next few days.

Then he has settled into bed, had rolled onto his side and waited for the morphine to make him feel sleepy or woozy, anything that might help him close his eyes. It hadn't. He'd doze for a few minutes and then wake up and check to see if Kitty had texted or called. He'd repeated this process several times, each time feeling more frustrated at his inability to sleep.

He was growing increasingly agitated, restless and fidgety. His head was swimming, and he felt sick to his stomach. He set his phone back on his bedside table, disconnected the bag of fluids from the line in his hand and forced himself to sit up. "Oh god," he groaned. He really was going to be sick. He scrambled out of bed to get to his bathroom. His legs gave out under him as he tried to stand, and he collapsed to the floor.
"Fuck," he cursed as he forced himself onto his hands and knees just in time to throw up onto the black rug he'd been given by his parents for Christmas. He coughed and heaved over and over as he tried to move to get a cloth. He used the bed to pull himself back up to his feet before promptly passing out and hitting the floor with a loud thud.

As Anthony slept, he felt something pressed against his body, his arm slightly too high but not uncomfortably so. Slowly, he opened his eyes and saw a mop of chocolate brown hair directly in front of his face. Then he realised it was Kitty he could feel. She was spooning against him, fast asleep, and his arm was draped over her. Content in the knowledge that she was safe and in his arms, he closed his eyes and went back to sleep.

The next time Anthony awoke, it was to the sound of distant noise. He didn't open his eyes; he just reached for Kitty. She was gone.

Shit.

He opened his eyes and sat up quickly, blinking and looking around the room. He couldn't see Kitty. The door to his bedroom was slightly open, but not enough that he could see into the living room.

"Kitty," he called. "Honey, are you here?"

"Hey you," she called from a distance. "Stay right there. I'll be with you in just a minute."

He adjusted his pillows against his headboard, leant back against them and picked up his phone. "What the hell?" he said as he looked at the time. How on earth was it almost half past five in the evening? He'd slept all day. Instantly unlocked his phone, and he began to check his emails. That was odd. He had a few personal ones but nothing on his school account.

"Hi," Kitty said.

Anthony looked up from his phone and gasped. Kitty was standing in his bedroom doorway in a black satin bra, a matching thong and one of his long-sleeved white shirts completely undone. She had bare feet, her hair was in a messy top knot on her head, and she was carrying a tray of tea and toast. She looked breathtaking.

"Hi yourself," he said, trying to focus on anything over than her semi-naked body and failing.

"I've been asleep all day," he said, still not quite believing it.

"Oh dear," Kitty frowned.

"What?" Anthony asked.

"Did you just check the time on your phone?" Kitty asked.

"Yes, why?" He really was puzzled, but he waved it lightly in the air at her.

"Did you happen to check the day and date?" she asked.

Anthony looked down at his phone again and then straight back up at Kitty.

"THREE DAYS?" he roared. "I've been asleep for three days?"

"Here we go again," Kitty said softly.

"Again?" Anthony really didn't enjoy being so confused, and he wanted to know what the heck was going on. "Did you pull a spell on me, Kitty?"

Kitty chuckled softly, set down the tray on what Anthony assumed had now become her bedside table and scooted onto the bed. She lay her head down on this lap, and it felt entirely natural for him to want to untie her top knot and stroke her loose hair, so he did.

"I didn't put a spell on you," she said finally.

"This may be hard for you to hear, my love, but I am going to tell it to you anyway."

"I'm ready," he told her as he began to gently tease her curls, wrapping them around his fingers.

"That first morning when we all got home, you just couldn't rest," Kitty told him. "You were still on a comedown after the night before and worked up that I hadn't been to see you yet. Sorry about that; by the way. I just needed to see my girls and spend some time with them before I did anything else. Anyway, you eventually accepted some morphine, but you didn't react very well to it. When the doctor came into check you at around half-eight, you were unconscious on the floor with your face in a puddle of puke."

"Oh delightful," he said sarcastically. "I bet I looked gorgeous."

"You always look gorgeous, babe," Kitty assured him before continuing. "When you finally came around, you were delirious and worked up. You'd had nightmares, and you were convinced the hostages were still missing. The doctor couldn't calm you down, so he had no option but to sedate you."

"I don't remember any of it," Anthony said, trying to force the memory to the surface. "I am glad you went to spend time with the girls, though, before coming to see me. That was absolutely the right move, and I'm sorry I never even thought that was where you might have been. I was just worried that something had happened at the scene."

Kitty nodded and patted Anthony's leg tenderly.

"From there," Kitty continued. "Every time you woke up, you became stressed, agitated and even aggressive. Doc thinks it might have been a bad reaction to the morphine he'd been giving you to keep on top of the pain. Like it was causing you to hallucinate and relive what happened to you on Monday. You kept panicking about Fitz, convinced he didn't make it. You kept asking to see his body, and you just wouldn't accept that Fitz is alive doing well."

"Fitz is good, though, right?" Anthony asked, suddenly anxious. "He's getting better, isn't he? And everyone else. Are they all doing O.K?"

"Fitz is recovering well," Kitty assured him. "He's being discharged tomorrow and going home with Jenny, who has hardly left his side. Clare is at home with her family and is coping quite well. All of the girls are with their families. Some have gone on family holidays to distract them, some are just resting at home. They all have a lot of psychological healing to do, but we've brought in a specialist team of people in to help them with that. They're going to be sticking around for quite a while to make sure everyone gets the support they need."

Relief washed over Anthony as he listened to Kitty. He felt guilty for not being there for everyone when they needed him to be a leader, but he knew something had happened to him and that he had also needed time to heal. He knew he wouldn't have been any good to anyone if he had tried to push himself to keep going in the state he was in. Yet, he still didn't fully understand what had happened to him.

"Do you want to hear the rest of your story now?" Kitty asked gently.

Anthony nodded. He needed her to finish filling in the gaps for him. He needed her to help him piece together the missing information and make sense of it.

"When you started to become aggressive and delusional, Doc and I talked things through," Kitty told Anthony. "We decided the safest option would be to keep you sedated so he could stop the morphine. The sedation was to help you to be calm and restful until after the morphine left your system and to help keep you pain-free."

"I see," Anthony said, wondering whether or not he really did see. He desperately wanted to remember it all, but he couldn't remember anything talking to Fitz's parents and worrying about where Kitty was.

"You were in a bad place, my love," Kitty said. "We needed to give you time to rest and heal safely."

"Was I really aggressive?" he asked. That didn't seem like him at all. Monday notwithstanding, he was usually relatively passive, and when he was worked up, he visited the gym or ran.

"Yeah, about that," Kitty said. "Doc said the combination of trauma and morphine made the hallucinations pretty bad, and at one point, you were really quite agitated. I'm afraid it came down to putting you in a binding spell or basically punching you out."

"Please tell me you punched me out," Anthony said. He did not like the thought of being some magical puppet, and he didn't like the idea of Kitty using her witchcraft on him anytime she chose to do so.

"Of course I punched you out," Kitty said. She rolled onto her front, looked up at Anthony and grinned. "With the exception of the blood to blood spell we used to track you when you were missing, I have never used any form of magic on you, and I never would."

"Really?" Anthony asked as he allowed his finger to trace the curves of her lips. "So then why do I feel like I'm under your spell Kitty Kline?"

"Oh, I'm pretty sure I'm under yours," Kitty said. "Or at least that's what my former unit thinks."

"Your former unit?" Anthony asked.

"I've handed in my notice," Kitty shrugged. "I'm resigning from the task force and from the military. You are caressing the lips of a retired General."

"But why?" Anthony asked, frowning. "You love your job Kitty, and you're amazing at it. Why would you just give it all up so suddenly?"

"I don't want my life to be dangerous anymore," Kitty said. "When I started doing this, it was because I needed something to make me feel closer to Jack and forget about him all at the same time. I don't need that anymore. I feel peaceful now. I've finally let go of all the shadows that were following me, and it took you to help me do it."

Anthony did not want to take the credit for that. It felt wrong to him that he should be the reason Kitty had stopped mourning for her husband, and he wasn't O.K. with that. He also wasn't O.K. with her walking away from her career either. Dangerous or not, it was a massive part of who she was, and he didn't want her to just walk away from that on a whim.

"How do Ivy and Rosie feel about that?" he asked.

"Relieved," she said. "We had a long talk about things. Including the fact that they have a few things, they have been keeping secret from me.

"Like What? Anthony asked.

Like twin telepathy and telekinesis," Kitty answered honestly.

"More magic," he sighed. Magic was going to take a lot of getting used to, that was for sure.

"I thought you might feel like that," Kitty said, smiling up at Anthony. "So, I've left you a present in the living room."

"What is it?" he asked, suddenly curious.

"It's a collection of articles and theses written over the years about the impact witchcraft has had on science, including some which aren't readily available in the public domain. Many were written scientists who have witnessed the supernatural abilities of witches and documented how it impacts our understanding of physics."

Anthony looked down at Kitty and smiled warmly.

"You got those for me?" he asked.

"Well, I know you love the learning," she said affectionately. "I thought these would help introduce you to my world from the point of view of your world."

"That was really thoughtful of you," Anthony said. "Thank you."

Anthony hoped that looking at the world of witchcraft from a scientific point of view would help him come to terms with his introduction to all things magic and mystery. He loved that Kitty had taken the time to arrange that for him. He loved that she didn't just expect him to understand and accept her world and that she felt it important for him to explore it comfortably.

"You didn't need to give up your career, though, Kitty," he said softly.

"This job was never my dream," she admitted.

"What is your dream job then?" Anthony asked. "I want a shop," she said. "I want my own little occult shop, and I want to teach young witches how to explore the craft safely and effectively." "Well, you know I strongly approve of educating young minds," he said. "If you need help designing a curriculum, just say."

Kitty beamed up at him. "I love you," she said. It was the first time Kitty had said it since the night in the warehouse. That he'd heard, at least. Anthony had wondered if when she said it that night, it was because she was caught up in the intense emotion of the situation. Part of him hadn't allowed himself it believe it was really true. Now though, she was here with her head on his lap, calmly talking about the future and she had told him she loved him. Did that mean he had a place in her future?

"I love you too," he said as he began to stroke her hair again. "I'll go anywhere to be with you, Kitty. Wherever you want. I can teach anywhere, but I want you to be where you and the girls are safe and settled."

"What are you saying?" Kitty asked, sitting up suddenly.

"I'm saying I want my life to be with you," he said. "I'm saying I want us to have a future and be a family. I'm saying I want to marry you."

"You're proposing to me?" she asked.

Anthony was just as surprised as she was. He hadn't made any sort of grand plan to propose. He hadn't even given it much thought. It was just something that he realised he wanted, and now he'd said it, he wanted it even more.

Anthony had waited too long to build a life with Kitty. He had denied the possibility that they could have any sort of life together for too many years. He wasn't going to waste another day. He wanted Kitty to be a part of his life for the rest of his life.

"I guess I am," he smiled at her. "What do you think? Want to marry this stuck up snob Kitty?"

"I do, Teach," Kitty said. "I really do."

Anthony rolled his eyes and then pulled her into his arms and kissed her.

Epilogue

It had been eighteen months since Anthony had proposed. Eighteen amazing months. As Kitty stood and looked in the full-size mirror in her bedroom, she still couldn't believe how much her life had changed. Everything about her life was so different from how it had been a year and a half ago.

She was no longer a single mother, hiding her identity or running from her feelings. She no longer worked with her counterterrorism task force. She no longer lived in that house in Surrey, and she no longer drove a high-tech S.U.V. with secret panels and flashing lights.

As of that morning, she was officially Kathryn Richmond. Her daughters were now Ivy and Rosie Richmond. She lived in a cottage in the New Forest, owned a thriving occult shop, was a teacher and mentor to young witches, and drove an old Land Rover that she absolutely loved.

She took one last look at herself in the mirror, smoothed down her white dress and headed over to the bed. It was the same bed that she had first shared with Anthony. That king-size mahogany bed that used to be in his quarters at Surrey Hills Prep and today it had that same bed linen on it.

Those first few nights in that bed together had been rough. Anthony had been alternating between the initial trauma of the events surrounding the S.W.O. kidnapping and being sedated. Kitty hadn't slept much at all during those first few nights as she had wanted to keep a close eye on him to make sure he was safe and resting. Yet, when he finally woke up, he had proposed to her on this bed, and her world had changed forever. He'd made love to her on top of those sheets and had held her in his arms under that duvet cover as they had talked and slept.

She sat, picked up his pillow, wrapped her arms around it and held it close to her as she breathed in his scent. She could feel that same photo in the pillowcase. He had insisted that it should remain under his pillow every night rather than going into a frame. It was how he had kept her close to him for so long, he'd told her.

"I'm coming for you, baby," she whispered as she gave the pillow one final squeeze and set it back down at the top of his side of the bed.

Then she stood, left the room and made her way down the stairs and into her kitchen.

She walked across the room and stopped at the back door of her little thatched-roof cottage, and took a breath. Excitement and nerves gripped her at the same time. She looked down at her long white, crocheted dress and then looked back up at her two beautiful daughters.

"Ready, Mum?" Ivy asked.

"Ready," Kitty said.

"Dad looks nervous too," Rosie said.

Kitty nodded and smiled.

"I bet he looks so handsome standing at the altar in his suit," Kitty smiled. "He said he'd brought a new one especially for this evening."

They had done the legal stuff with a ceremony at the registry office that morning. It had been just Kitty, Anthony, Rosie and Ivy, along with Jenny and Fitz as witnesses.

From there, they had gone to family court, where Anthony's adoption of the girls had been finalised, and they had legally changed their names. They were now Ivy Richmond and Rosie Richmond, daughters of Anthony and Kathryn Richmond.

Now, as Kitty and the girls stood in her back garden, she took a moment to reflect on how content she felt. She had her daughters, her cottage in the New Forest, her little occult shop with a room in the back for teaching and a second room for one to one work with clients. The final step was to walk down the aisle and meet her man at the altar, where they would be joined together in a handfasting ceremony.

"Let's do this," she said at last.

She leant in and hugged each of her girls. Then they set off out of the back gate and into the forest where they would make their way down the aisle to where Anthony waited. Then she walked to Peter, who was waiting for her at the gate.

"You look beautiful, Kitty," he said as he handed her a bouquet of lavender, poppies and daisies, all of which Kitty had grown in her own garden.

"I can't believe it's finally happening," she said to Peter as she slipped her arm into his. "I can't believe I have been blessed with everything I ever dreamed of and so much more."

"Believe it, Kitty," he said. "This is real. This is happening right now, and you deserve every glorious moment of it.

In the distance, Kitty could hear the beginning chords of Air on a G String. Peter cringed.

"Oh yay," he teased. "More classical music. God, you're old Kitty."

"Or just well cultured," she said.

"Just like a yoghurt," he laughed.

"Fuck off, Peter," Kitty snapped before she burst out laughing.

"You ready?" he asked.

"I'm ready," she said.

"Let's go get your man Peter said as he led her through the gate and into the forest.

"I'm glad you're here, Sir," she whispered as they walked toward the ceremony space that had been put together in the forest for the handfasting.

"Don't call me Sir," Peter told her playfully. "You know you still outrank me."

Peter resigned from the police and stayed with Kitty's former task force fulltime after the events eighteen months earlier. He was the only one of the primary members of the team who didn't have supernatural abilities. Still, he had years of tactical experience, good connections with police forces across the country and had even learnt to spell cast.

Kitty teased him about being the new kid in town at fifty, but the truth was she was very proud of him and knew he was a fantastic asset to her old team.

As they reached the top of the aisle, Kitty paused to look at the sea of faces watching her.

Thorpe was there with a heavily pregnant Nikki holding his hand. Fitz, now the headteacher at S.H.P., was there with Jenny, who was now his wife. Clare, Chris, Bo and several of Anthony's former colleagues and students were also there. Kitty's former coven and Rocket Man sat near the front of the aisle. Kate was standing at the altar waiting to perform the ceremony as the coven's new high priestess and the task force's new commanding officer. Even her old neighbour Betty and her kids were there. Finally, right at the front of the aisle were Anthony's parents and sisters, who had welcomed Kitty, Rosie and Ivy with open arms and gladly made them part of the family.

Then finally, she stepped forward, and she saw him. Anthony.

Anthony who was not wearing a suit at all, but instead wearing black linen slacks, a white linen shirt and black flip flops. He looked gorgeous. She couldn't believe it, he wasn't wearing a suit. He hadn't really worn a suit for quite some time, and it turned out he owned many pairs of jeans. Yet, he'd told Kitty he was really looking forward to finally putting on a suit again for the ceremony.

He looked at her, and Kitty felt everyone else around her disappear. She wasn't sure how long they stood there looking at each other, but she was finally brought back to reality by the sound of Peter clearing his throat.

Kitty looked up at Peter and then looked at her two beautiful daughters, who had been waiting at the top of the aisle for her. She hugged each of them, kissed their heads and then watched as they walked down the aisle to where Anthony was waiting.

Then as Kitty started walking down the aisle to Anthony, she knew she was finally stepping into the future with Anthony she had dreamed of for almost nine years.

When they reached the end, Peter kissed her cheek before placing her hand in Anthony's and taking his place beside his wife, Sarah. Kitty watched Peter sit before turning her attention to Anthony.

"You look gorgeous, Ant," she said softly.

"And look breath-taking Mrs Richmond," he whispered.

"Where's your suit?" She asked.

"There's something I need to tell you about that," Anthony told her.

She leaned closer to him so that he could whisper in her ear.

"Tell me," she breathed.

"I really fucking hate suits, Kitty," he said against her ear.

Kitty laughed out loud and wrapped her arms around Anthony.

"I love you," he said.

"I love you too, baby," she told him.

"Marry me, Kitty," Anthony whispered. "Will you marry me right now?"

"Yes, Anthony," Kitty said softly. "I'll marry you right now."

Acknowledgements

There are so many people I want to thank for supporting me while I wrote this book.

- ❖ My beautiful daughters, Roo, Daisy, Ella and Autumn.
  Thank you for putting up with me while I spent weeks squirreled away writing, rather than being a fun mum. I know you have had to spend a lot of time hanging out with me on my bed and have put up with many hours of me isolating myself to get this written. Thank you for not being too mad at me and for still loving me. You are my everything and I love you to the moon and back.
- ❖ Warren.
  Thank you for working all day, then cooking dinner and taking care of the kitchen for weeks while I basically left you in charge of everything to write. I'm so sorry that you had to spend many evenings on your own while I was being anti-social. I am going to try to be better at time keeping and show some self-restraint in the future. Honest, I am! I love you and appreciate everything you do, more than you know.

- ❖ Rebekah, Nyree-Dawn, Ocean, Jo, Emma and Hayley – My coven, my sisters, my best friends.

  Thank you for putting up with countless messages about my book progress and those seriously naughty thoughts about chapter 14! Thank you for encouraging me, supporting me and for being there for me in those moments when I doubted my ability to get this book finished. You are the best friends any witch could ever want and I am proud to call you my sisters. I hope this book was worth the wait. I love you queens.

- ❖ Alastair McKenzie.

  Thank you for letting me sit in the car park for hours on end so that I could write in peace while the girls were in homework club, detention or at the park. Also, thank you for not pointing out just how weird I am for sitting in my car for hours every single day. If it helps, I already know.

- ❖ Michelle Lim.

  Thanks for the brownie and rocky road. You know which day I'm talking about! Sometimes a friendly ear and chocolate are all a girl needs to pick herself up and shake her tail feathers. Given how many emails I send you on a weekly basis, are you surprised I managed to finish this? On a bright side, at least they aren't randy emails!!!

❖ Kevin Broadway.
How could I not take a moment to thank the man who helped turn me into a drama queen and who always encouraged my love of literature and all things dramatic? Thank you for your patience, kindness, support and for not locking me in the drama cupboard and throwing away the key. You inspired me more than you know, and you're the reason I love to write about teachers. I may not have been the best student, but you were the best teacher. More than twenty years later, I am honoured to call you my friend.

❖ Maurice John
Thank you so much for taking the time to talk to me as I struggled to find a way to write about the racism issues so many people around us face on a daily basis. I really wanted to highlight this in a way that wasn't disrespectful to the black community, and I hope I succeeded, with your help. I also hope I wasn't offensive to women and the LQBTQ+ community either. As a bisexual woman, I hope I have enough experience to be able to write

about the issues women and the LGBTQ+ community face with authority. As a white woman, I knew I wouldn't be able to write about the racism problem this world faces and must put an end to, without some help. I'm really grateful you were so willing to step up and be that help. Thank you so much for your help and support. I really hope I haven't let you down.

A letter from Stace

Dearest reader

Thank you for buying my book, I really hope you enjoyed it. A lot of blood, sweat and tears went into writing this. Papercuts!

When writing this book, I really wanted to highlight some of the key problems our country continues to face on a daily basis. Terrorism, racism, sexism and homophobia. As a bisexual woman, I hope I have been able to write with some authority about the issues women and the LGBTQ+ face. However, as I white woman, I was very nervous about writing about racism.

I am very grateful to have a really good friend who was so willing to speak to me about the racism he has been subjected to over the years as a black man. He was kind enough to advise and guide me as I tried to write this story in a way that wouldn't be offensive.

While this book tells an extreme story, it does highlight some of the real-life problems in our society, and I hope it will encourage all of us to do better. However, I sincerely apologise if this book has caused offence to any women or members of the black and LGBTQ+ communities.

I really enjoyed playing around with the character names in this book. It is the start of a pattern for my heroes. In this book, my hero was Anthony. In my next book, my hero is called Benedict. In 2022, my heroes will be called Cameron, Darcy, Edward, Frances and Garret. I hope you can see the pattern that is emerging there.

While there is so much more I would love to share with you, I'm writing this in the middle of the night in a desperate bid to meet my writing targets. Therefore, it is time for me to sign off and do to bed.

Thank you so much for purchasing this book. I look forward to sharing my new PTA novella series with you soon.

Blessed be.

Stace xoxo

Social Media

I would love to hear from you. Why not reach out to me on one of my social media platforms or by email? Here's how you can get in touch.

Twitter: @StaceWoods_

Instagram: @woodsstace

Email: woodsstace@gmail.com

My blog: www.stacewoods.com

I'd love to read your review of The Secret General on Amazon too. Reviews really help authors to find new readers. Thank you.

Meet the author

Stace Woods lives in Surrey, England with her long-time partner and her four wonderful daughters. She also has two tech-mad step sons who she adores. Stace is the chairperson of her kids' school PTA, and her life mostly revolves around school runs, school meetings and detentions.

In the nineteen years Stace has been a parent, her children and step children have attended ten schools. She has a wealth of experience with different schools, different PTAs and different headteachers. Therefore, she decided to about write what she knows; school life.

Stace is also obsessed with all things witchcraft and couldn't write her first novel without including a witchy storyline.

Stace has Fibromyalgia and suffers with Fibro brain and a short attention span. She feels it was a miracle that she was ever able to pen a sixty-five thousand word novel, especially as it was only supposed to be a twenty-five thousand word novella.

She is currently working on a six part novella series about a fictitious school PTA, with no witchcraft or magic involved. At some point, she'd like to write a story about a farm.

COMING SOON

2021
Christmas with the PTA

2022
Valentine's Day with the PTA
Springtime with the PTA
Summer with the PTA
Halloween with the PTA
New Year's Eve with the PTA

Printed in Great Britain
by Amazon

68969027R00197